I0557092

Memories, Why?

Stories, memories and mental meanderings

Michael Davies
a Couple of Old Blokes and some young friends

Memories, Why?

All Rights Reserved

Copyright © 2012 Michael Davies

Illustrations © by Brian Andrews

Reproduction in any manner, in whole or in part,
in English or any other language, or otherwise,
without the written permission of the copyright holder is
. prohibited

This is a work of fiction.
All characters and events portrayed in the book are fictional.
Any resemblance to real persons or events is purely coincidental.

For information address: mickiedaltonbooks@lycos.com

First Published in 2016 in Australia

ISBN: 978-0-9944523-6-8

Published by The Mickie Dalton Foundation
NSW
Australia

www.mickiedaltonfoundation.com

Other Books by Michael Davies

For Adults

The Nightmares of God
The Janus Conspiracy
Ready, Steady, KILL!
Helix Dreams

A Friendly Killing
Dreamkill
Accounts of a Killing

The Business School Approach to Writing Your Novel
(non-fiction)

For Children & Young Adults

The Many Worlds of Mickie Dalton
The Many Galaxies of Mickie Dalton
The Many Universes of Mickie Dalton
(Trilogy written with the students of St Joseph's Catholic High School, Albion Park)

The Julie Malloy Gang and the Smugglers
The Secret of Charlotte's Cello
(written with the children of Rollands Plains Upper Public School)

The Red Fog of Time
(written with the students of Comboyne Public School)

The Mysterious Recorder and the Door to Elsewhere
(written with the students of Gladstone Public School)

The Quest for the Locket
(written with the students of Comboyne Public School)

The Secret of Yuri Kirilenko
(written with the students of Byabarra Public School)

The United Nations and the Extra-Terrestrial
(written with a group of Burundian, Sudanese and Aboriginal children at the Coffs Harbour Neighbourhood Centre, NSW)

The Star of the Yshan Kings
The War of the Yshan Empire
The Star of the New Yshan Empire
(Trilogy written with the students of Willawarrin Public School)

The Strange World of Mark and Anna
(Written with the students of Bishop Druitt Anglican College, Coffs Harbour)

A Step into the Past
(Written with the students of Taree West Public School)

Mary's World
(For the 3-5 year olds)

Contents

Stories from the Kids

The Fairy Visitation

I took the seat in the booth of Lou's Diner, relishing the idea of my monthly breakfast routine of cholesterol overload, a leisurely scanning of the newspaper reports of the world's foibles and horrors and a break from the increasing workload. My order given, I unfolded *"The Australian"* and relaxed.

"Mind if I join you?"

Irritated, I looked up. Some, if not all the irritation faded as I looked at the uncommonly attractive young woman standing at the edge of the booth. But it wasn't all gone and she seemed to understand it.

"It's important," she said. "I really do need to talk to you."

Suppressing both my annoyance and my curiosity, I gestured at the seat across from me and folded away the paper.

"So what's so important that a complete stranger has to interrupt my breakfast? You're not serving legal papers or anything like that, are you?"

She chuckled. It was a nice sound and I wondered if I could make it happen again. She placed her handbag on the bench and smoothed down the nicely filled blue blouse that showed some distracting curves.

"Nothing like that," she replied. "Quite the reverse, in fact. I'm here to grant you three wishes."

"Huh?"

She laughed more loudly and it sounded even prettier than the chuckle. "That's the usual reaction!" she said. "But honest, you're getting your three wishes today!"

I decided to play along, more in the hope I could make her laugh again than any belief in what she was saying.

"Why?" I asked.

"The Council decided," she said.

"What Council?"

"The one that decides who gets their three wishes."

This time it was my turn to laugh and looked around for the camera. "Candid Camera?" I asked. "Or The Chaser's War on Everything?"

"Neither. Why don't you just go with the flow here and make your three wishes? I've got two more of these today and the others are quite some way away."

"How far?" Something about her was getting to me. There was a power in her, something radiating.

"One in Florida, one in Kharbarovsk."

"All in one day?"

"Sure, why not? Fairies don't go by regular airlines, you know."

I let this settle inside my head. Something about her....

"Can I ask you a couple of questions?"

"Sure."

"My breakfast will be here soon. Do you want anything?"

She shook her head. "I don't eat or drink. Anyway, she won't see me."

I felt a slight shiver. The waitress chose that moment to arrive and place my coffee mug and loaded plate on the table. She didn't look at the pretty woman in the opposite seat.

"See?" said the girl. "Nobody can hear us, either."

I lifted my knife and fork and cut into the bacon to give me time to think.

"That stuff isn't good for you," she said with a smile.

"It's my monthly pig-out."

She nodded. "That's okay then. Now, these questions?"

I lifted the bacon and hash brown into my mouth and chewed carefully. When it had gone down, I sipped at the coffee, struggling to arrange my thoughts. *This was silly...*

"Why am I getting this honour? I can't think of anything wildly worthy that I've done."

She shrugged her pretty shoulders.

"No specific thing. Rather a cumulative result of lots of things. Like the time you wheeled that black guy in Chicago in his wheelchair a couple of miles to get his bus to New York."

"Good grief!" I'd forgotten that. I remembered that he'd looked fatigued and not well and it was nearly freezing.

"And lending your apartment in Toronto to a middle-aged woman who'd been abandoned by her husband and left homeless."

"Just little things," I said, feeling embarrassed.

"They mount up."

I shuffled the sausage around the scrambled eggs and carefully built a forkful of calories.

"There have always been stories about people asking somebody like you for a wish and it gets granted but with awfully literal interpretations. Do you try and do that?"

"What, like asking to be irresistible to women and being changed into a baby?"

I nearly choked on my just-loaded mouthful of hash browns and bacon. "That sort of thing!" I agreed once I had recovered.

"You've got to be precise," she replied.

"Or asking for world peace and finding everybody in the world is dead."

"Like I said, be careful what you wish for."

"Will you warn me if I wish for something that could have a terrible interpretation?"

"No."

"Don't you worry about what people will ask for?"

She shrugged. "In the long term, it doesn't matter."

"Long term?"

"I've been doing this for about a thousand years and my contract goes on another thousand."

I sat back, breakfast forgotten. I tried to ignore the implications of what she had said.

"Okay, let's try this. For the next State Lottery which I choose to enter, I'll be the single and only winner of the first prize."

"That'll work," she said. "Otherwise you might have won the first prize with ten thousand other people and got perhaps a thousand bucks. What will you do with the $31 Million you're going to win?"

Feeling calmer, I dug back into the calorie fiesta on my plate. I probably had it straight now. I still didn't believe her story, though.

"Give most of it away," I said. "I don't really need that sort of wealth, but lots of friends and some family need help."

I received a nice smile for that. *Just the most kissable mouth I have ever seen...*

She chuckled and I had the embarrassing sensation that she'd read my thoughts.

"I did," she said. "Thank you."

I took my time taking another sip of my coffee. My doubts about her were fast fading.

"Second wish," I said. "Over the next year, my body shape will return to the one it had when I started the second year of my Master's degree back in 1977 and stay like that the rest of my life."

"Easy," she said. "And last?"

"Do you enjoy doing this?" I asked.

Her eyes widened. "Sometimes," she said. "Not always. Too often, people cause horrible problems out of greed and stupidity."

"Why do you do it?"

"I have to, and don't ask me why, I can't explain any of it."

"Something you did once and you have to do something in return?"

She nodded, her face expressionless.

"So what would be your wish if you could have anything you wanted?"

"To move on to the next stage of existence, and again, don't ask me to explain."

But I saw it. "Does that mean you were once a human being?"

She nodded and I saw tears in her eyes. Everything became very simple.

"Can I assign one of my wishes to you?"

I saw the sudden hope in her eyes and she nodded.

"Then my third wish is that you can have your wish and move onto the next stage of existence," I said.

She touched my hands and vanished.

Newspaper forgotten, I took out my pen and began planning what to do with $31 Million dollars. But I would never forget those lovely lips.

The Sci-Fi Writer

My teachers were always going on about what an imagination I had. At school, that always seemed to be a good thing because I could do great essays and short stories and stuff like that, but it wasn't much good with maths and physics. My physics teacher said it would actually be fantastically useful thing if I wanted to go into something called theoretical physics, but I'd need to be seriously good at maths and I wasn't.

My parents weren't too excited by this imagination thing. Mum just reads those crappy romances and smokes. Dad's a chemist, works in oil refining or something over at Kurnell and it's obvious that it bugs him that I'm always reading books. I've never seen him read anything except the newspaper and sometimes he stops by where I'm sitting, grabs my book off me and stares at it.

"What's this rubbish?" he'd say.

"It's Asimov," I said the last time. "It's about robots."

"It's bloody rubbish!" he shouted and threw the book into the corner. "Get up to your room and do your homework!"

I knew if I argued, I'd get a beating. So I went up to my room and opened a couple of books on my desk and read another sci-fi book, keeping the draw open so I could slide it in there if I heard the stairs creak. I'd done my homework before he even got home from work.

Then one Saturday, I took my book to the Harbour and

walked round from Rose Bay to a tiny private beach I'd found. Nobody had ever come down the path from the house high up on the hill so I felt pretty safe. And there I was reading my *"Foundation"* book by Asimov when somebody did come down the hill.

She looked about eighteen and she was really pretty, wearing a tee shirt and blue denim shorts. I couldn't help but stare at her and she grinned.

"Hello!" she said in a friendly sort of way. She didn't seem to mind that I was there or that I was staring at her.

I closed the book, feeling worried. If she called the cops I'd get the biggest beating of my life from my dad.

"Don't worry," she said, as if she could read what I was thinking. "I'm just leaving."

I wondered why she would come all the way down that hill if she was going to leave again right away. But I heard this odd sound out in the water and I turned round to see this weird little boat just seem to lift out from under the surface about twenty metres away. It looked like a tiny submarine, a conning tower and all, just like all the pictures I'd seen. But then it got even weirder, because a door sort of opened in the middle of that conning tower and I couldn't see anything inside because it was filled with a blue light that made me close my eyes it was so glaring.

"Okay, see you, Phil," the pretty girl said. "I'm going now."

"How did you know my name?" I asked, feeling that everything was just a bit too strange and wondering if I was having a dream.

"Easy," she replied. "And don't worry about having that wild imagination. It's much better than being like your dad and it will be a great advantage when you grow up."

I just stared at her and then it got even more crazy because she just floated out over the water, landed by the blue doorway and walked inside. Just as she was about to close the door, she looked back at me with a lovely smile. "Yes I am. About nine hundred light years away," she said.

And I'd been wondering if she was an alien and where she came from. Then I realised that somehow she'd read my thoughts. The door closed, cutting off that blue glare and the little boat sunk under the surface without a ripple.

I just sat there till nearly dark feeling terribly sad because I knew I'd never see her again. Eventually I walked home. When I walked in at the back door, Mum was cooking something, a cigarette hanging from the corner of her mouth, her eyes squinted against the smoke. I really hated that.

"Where have you been," she mumbled, spilling ash from the cigarette onto the kitchen floor.

"Rose Bay," I said. "I met an alien girl from nine hundred light years away and she got into a small submarine and disappeared."

"Don't be stupid," she muttered. "And better not tell your dad, you know how he hates the way you make things up. That stupid imagination of yours, it's going to get you into a lot of trouble one day."

Yes, mum," I said and went to my room. I knew I'd dream of that girl for the rest of my life and wished that she'd come back and see me when I was a bit older. I also knew I'd never tell anyone about the meeting but I couldn't wait till the weekend when I could walk round to that beach again.

International Expert Solves Problem of Missing Livestock

Police are investigating the mysterious disappearance of some fifty sheep that vanished without trace from a paddock near Gladstone, NSW. The shepherdess, Ms Bodelicious Peep (17), daughter of Hiram and Ariadne Peep of South West Rocks and known to her friends as Bo said that she had led the flock into the paddock at 6:30am and at some stage realised that they had vanished.

An immediate search failed to find the missing livestock and fears were held for their safety.

Local CID officers called on assistance from internationally renowned Chinese-Israeli veterinarian, Professor Shlomo Wong. He said that it was almost certain that Ms Peep had fallen asleep on the job, allowing the sheep to wander off, despite her denials.

"However," said Professor Wong. "Sheep are naturally homing creatures of habit and they will quite certainly find their way back within a day or two, unless they encounter a predator."

This is, in fact, what happened, and two days after the disappearance, the flock returned to the paddock, missing only one animal.

Ms Peep was charged in South West Rocks Juvenile Court with endangering the livestock and was given a suspended sentence of six months plus six weeks of community service, doing evening strip shows at the Kempsey Boys Club.

Spooks

"Mind if I take a seat?"

The elderly man sitting on the park bench looked up from his contemplation of the view over the Hastings River to the sea. A man of about his own age was standing at the end of the bench, smiling politely. He was dressed much like him as well, casual slacks, golf shirt, sneakers. They could have been members of the same bowling team from the local country club.

"Sure," said the seated man and moved over nearer the arm rest, leaving plenty of space for the newcomer who took a place next to the other end.

"Beautiful day," said the new arrival. "I've always liked this view. I'm Ken Bradshaw."

"Barry Smith," said the other man and waved across the distance, too great to shake hands.

"Retired like me, I suppose?" said Ken.

"Yes," said Barry. "Forty years in engineering, it's nice to be free."

"Hmm. So, tell me Yuri Michailovich Petrov, just what are you *really* doing?"

The man called Barry froze and slowly turned his face to the other man who was watching him carefully. "Who the hell are you?" he croaked painfully.

"The opposition," replied Ken.

"I don't know what you're talking about," rasped Barry. "I'm a Lithuanian originally. I came here in the early fifties as a refugee."

"And very good forged papers you had," said Ken. "They almost fooled us then, but not quite. But you're Yuri Michailovich Petrov, ex-KGB, possibly still a Russian spook but now with the SVR."

The man called Barry seemed almost catatonic. He stared out over the river, his breathing shallow, his face white.

"The SVR?" he finally said, almost in a whisper.

"Still trying, eh?" said Ken. "The *Sluzhba vneshney razvedki*, the Foreign Intelligence Service of the Russian Federation, responsible for intelligence and espionage activities outside Russia. But you know that, Yuri, you're part of it."

Petrov slumped as if somebody had let go of the strings holding him up.

"So why did you let me enter Australia if you knew who I was?"

"Because it was obvious your mob was up to something. Better to let you in and watch you carefully than have you working up something ugly where we couldn't see you."

"And have you been watching me ever since?"

"Watching you? Damn right. I had you in my gun sights a couple of times and it was hard to stop myself pulling the trigger."

"You personally?"

"Me personally. You've been my biggest assignment all these years."

"Then you must be *Gonchaya.*"

"My code name was Beagle?" Ken let out a short laugh. "How very appropriate! I like it. I've certainly been tracking you for many years."

"But you have never seen me doing anything dangerous, have you? Does it occur to you that I might be just what I say I am, a refugee from Soviet tyranny?"

"Not a chance, Petrov. I was watching one evening when you met the ship returning from the UK. It was one of those ships used to transport tallow from here to Europe. Damn clever, I thought. The ships come back with a couple of feet of tallow still in the holds and somewhere near Indonesia, the Captain warms up the fat so it liquefies, a helicopter flies out, drops a load of weapons into the tanks, all nicely wrapped up and buried in solidified fat. Then when the tanks get steam cleaned back in Sydney, the weapons get taken to one of your storage places. You're in it up to your neck, Yuri, stop trying to bullshit me."

"And you know where we stored those guns then?" There was a trace of mockery in Petrov's voice.

"The warehouse in Armidale? Of course. We've had that under surveillance from the first shipment and we've seen five more go in there."

Petrov was silent, staring out over the river.

"So we're pretty sure we know what you're up to, you and your ugly friends, Yuri. The Saudis buy millions of dollars worth of weaponry from you and fund the Indonesians to train and prepare an invasion force. In return, the Saudis promise to give Russia first options on oil supplies and starve the Yanks. Then the Indonesians one day let loose all the fighting men they've been training, bring them secretly into Australia, hand out the guns and they take over. What's the plan? Take over Canberra and all the military HQ operations so you freeze the military?"

Petrov looked shaken. "That's about it," he said. "And do it on a Sunday or over Christmas or on Melbourne Cup day when the whole country is relaxed. We kidnap the entire political and military leadership and stand down the armed forces. Maybe behead the prime minister and chief of armed forces on the steps of Parliament House to show we mean business."

"Did you think about what the Americans would do?"

"The Americans!" Petrov spat into the ground at his feet. "They'd be too worried about offending Saudi Arabia and the rest of Islam to do anything and risk the oil deliveries, and anyway, a couple of major attacks on New York and Washington would distract them."

"And now it's over," said Ken. "You'll spend the rest of your life in one of our nasty little prisons the world doesn't know about, Armidale gets emptied out and a few sharp words go to the Indonesian president to tell him to back off or we might sink a few of his ships by accident."

"Are you wired?" asked Yuri.

"Of course. There's a truck just down the road, been listening to every word. You?"

"I didn't know you were coming. How could I be wired?"

"Fair enough, I suppose. Shall we go, Yuri?"

In the white van a kilometre away, the voices were soft.

"So they got Armidale," said the one obviously in charge. "But it seems they missed Queanbeyan, Flemington, Richmond and Dubbo."

"Still plenty enough for the plan," said his subordinate.

"Indeed," said the leader. "Contact Moscow and advise them to get Jakarta ready, activate all the troops. Australia will soon be a new Islamist state."

The other man nodded and started the engine.

("Spooks" was developed as an exercise in plot generation in a writing class that I ran at Camp Creative and other locations. During that exercise, we tried other variations on two men sitting on a park bench and while we didn't develop them to any great extent, they gave me the opening for several stories. These follow later in the book)

Muffy's Terrible Experience

A strange episode concerning a huge spider was reported in the science magazines last week. Apparently, a young child, Miss Arabella Muffet (8), known to her friends as Muffy had taken her lunchtime meal of curds and whey and was sitting on a school bench watching the boys' team playing football. She suddenly noticed an extraordinarily large spider sitting on the bench next to her.

"I was utterly terrified," said Muffy to our science reporter, Ms Booby McJugs. "I've never seen a spider so huge! But it just sat there, I think it wanted my lunch."

From the description that Muffy was able to give, Arachnologists decided it was probably a Bolivian Giant Bird-eating Tarantula *(Theraphosa Blondi Bolivaris)* which normally grows to a maximum of fifteen centimetres span, but Muffy insisted it was at least four times that size.

"I just upped and ran," she said, still looking frightened as she relived the appalling nightmare.

The school has conducted a major exercise of spraying the buildings and grounds and hopefully there will be no repeat of this extraordinary experience.

La Guardia Fantasy

I picked up my bag from the pile vomited forth by the X-ray machine, and became aware of a woman standing by my side, waiting for her own bag. Every sense in me reacted to her appearance. A couple of inches shorter than I, she was trim, neatly dressed in a suit with a skirt that was enchantingly abbreviated. A blue blouse had a high collar that was gently touched by light-brown hair snugly round her head. Her eyes were green. The face seemed to reflect confidence, composure. Something about her shape made me draw in my breath sharply.

"Oh my!" I said to myself. The strength of my reaction shook me. It wasn't that she was beautiful. It was her elegance, her sheer femininity. Confused, I walked on to the departure lounge. My sexual self-esteem was not up to coping with the emotions racing through me.

At Gate Seven, I sat down alongside one wall and took a deep breath. The woman had not appeared, and I felt oddly relieved that she would not be on my flight. I took my newspaper from my briefcase and read the article on the Internet again. I would pass it around my team in the morning.

My senses told me before my eyes did. She appeared in the corridor leading into the lounge carrying just a handbag. Despite my efforts not to, I couldn't help but stare at her. Her legs were beautiful. Her left hand was bare of rings. She gave me a single, cool glance and walked past, taking a seat at the other side of the lounge. Angry at myself, I felt depressed. There had been little happiness in recent years. The women I'd met had all seemed angry, determined to make any man they met suffer for the crimes of previous men. There seemed little joy in the contact. Two women had shared some part of my life over the past five years. Each had irritated me for one reason or another. Too loud, too insensitive or, in one case, too desperate. *Like me, now, perhaps.* The sex had been flat, without joy, without excitement. And the last two or three years, as my weight went up and my esteem went down, I had relegated myself to the hideous fate of being the nice, intelligent man with no sex appeal at all.

I returned to the paper and tried not to look across the lounge.

I failed. I looked up in her direction. She was standing up, re-arranging her jacket. Her figure was intensely disturbing. Something about it sent waves of need through me. The short skirt was perfect, fitting neatly round her small waist, ending four or five inches above the knees.

I rose to my feet, put my paper down and walked over to her.

"This is not a thing I usually do," I said to her surprised face. "But we have thirty minutes before our flight. Could I buy you a drink?"

19

She smiled at me. "That seems an excellent idea." Her voice was low and husky. The accent was charmingly English, southern counties, I judged. Her perfume sent subtle signals to my libido.

"Good," I said. "The bar is just up the corridor."

"I know," she said with a warm smile and tucked her hand in my arm as I turned away. Her head came just to my shoulder. "Why didn't you ask me at the security check-in?"

I smiled at her, and her eyes glowed. "Too shy," I said, laughing softly.

"Not a chance," she retorted. "And it was obvious then that we have something....."

I dropped my paper and realised I was staring at her. She was looking across the lounge at me with a diffident expression as if wondering if I was going to be a problem.

Furious at myself, I picked up the paper again, feeling a flush of embarrassment. *The lounge was too hot, dammit...* I had printers' ink on my fingers and I felt grubby. *When will you learn?* I demanded of myself. *Women like that aren't interested in men like you. They want tall, rich men who can be guaranteed to treat them like shit and make them feel feminine and victimised.* Savagely, I folded the paper away. I'd never be able to concentrate on network computers, Java programming languages and Microsoft's recent developments.

She had sat down again, and was looking into some private distance. *Dreaming about her rich, tall, abusive lover,* I swore to myself.

I looked around the seating area. A young Chinese girl was studying a technical manual of some sort in the row of seats across from me. She was dressed in loose, baggy jeans, and her hair was down to her waist. Two middle-aged men a few seats down from me were discussing some problem at their office. It seemed to involve disagreements on marketing policies. A thirty-something couple sat together, seemingly ignoring each other while they read books. She looked sad, dull. He seemed coarse, his mouth was open, thick lips moved slightly. The man coughed without shielding the output from the rest of the lounge.

Another business type sat, looking uncomfortable in his dark suit, talking with what seemed to be his wife. She was solid, unselfconscious, her handbag firmly on her knees, apparently lecturing her husband. They sat just behind.... I was looking at her again, and she was looking back. Her green eyes were fixed firmly on my face, but she wore no expression.

I smiled at her, and to my delight, she smiled back. Her green eyes were bright. I saw that the businessman and his wife had seen the interchange. The woman looked angry. The man looked distressed. You missed out, pal. He who dares, wins. I stood up and began to walk...

I looked away, angry at myself again. *Why didn't you smile at her, for God's sake? Christ, you never know, she might have smiled back, you could have manoeuvred yourself to be next to her when they called the flight, you could have somehow sat next to her, the flight's barely half full...* When I looked up again, she was delving into her handbag. The flight attendants were shuffling around the door as the first passengers walked out from the arriving flight. I lost sight of her as the line of arrivals became a thick flood. It had been a full flight from Toronto. Suddenly she smiled, that wide, delighted smile of seeing somebody who really mattered. She walked up to the tall, handsome man in the dark suit and they embraced passionately before walking out of the arrivals lounge to the streets of la Guardia.

I picked up my paper and tried to concentrate on Apple Computer's latest release.

An Old Love

I hadn't been in a primary school for years. Not since I'd last taken my daughter to hers and that must be thirty years ago or maybe more. I tried to stifle the usual thought of "Where had the years gone?" and looked around. Kids ran everywhere, harried-looking teachers seemed in constant panic and large numbers of parents stood around in small discussion groups. I imagined they'd all known each other from these meetings.

"Hey, grandad, this my pal, Jake!" My grandson Jason suddenly appeared before me with a small, red-haired boy who looked like he'd just gone ten rounds of combat with a mud pile.

"G'day, Jake!" I said and gravely shook his hand. It could have confused him, but I'd always been able to relate to kids and this one thawed immediately.

"Are you really Jason's grandad?" he asked. "Are you the one that writes books?"

"I really am, to both!" I replied.

He grinned. "I'm here with my grandma. She's over there! Hey, Gran!" he yelled over the loud hum of conversation.

I saw the slim, elegant woman turn and something hit me in the gut. But I knew her! Surely I knew her? I watched as she moved gracefully in my direction. Something about the walk... the athlete, the relaxed stride...

"Hello," she said. "I'm Mary Peterson. Jake says you're the author of some of the books in the school library?"

I looked into dark, serene eyes. Memories flooded back. She'd worn a fringe back in those days, the style of the sixties and the eyes had always seemed to smile, just as they did now.

I took a breath. "Yes, I am. I'm Patrick Henderson."

I saw the reaction in her.

"Patrick... Patrick Henderson! I thought you looked familiar! My God, Patrick! How long has it been?"

"Over fifty years, Mary. We were thirteen when we met at Palmer Park Hall in those square dances."

Her gaze drilled into my eyes. "I can't believe it! Patrick! You were the love of my life!"

"It was mutual, Mary. And I don't think I've ever gone more than a few days since then without thinking of you. What happened? Why did we break up?"

The room was forgotten, it had vanished. There was only that calm, serene face with the large, dark eyes in which I had once lost myself as a thirteen-year old.

"Patrick, I don't really know. But I think I was frightened. It was all too sudden, too intense. I couldn't handle it."

"And what happened to you?"

She touched her eye in which there was tiny glint of a tear.

"The usual. High school, nursing school, marriage, couple of kids. How about you?"

"The usual. University, the business world, marriage, a couple of kids. I wrote a few books and they seemed to have been successful."

She laughed. "Oh, you're that Patrick Henderson! Jake loves your work! You know, a couple of times I wondered if you could be the Patrick I knew, but decided it couldn't be."

"It was a late development. Were you happy with your usual existence?"

"Mostly. Do you know, I used to think about how we'd have been if we'd got married?"

I took a deep breath. "I did the same. Was your marriage a good one?"

She closed her eyes for a second. "I suppose. We didn't ever fight. But in the end, there wasn't any great passion, either. He's a surgeon, he provided a good home for me and the kids, I was a good wife. Still am. How about you?"

"Not so good. We didn't last and I didn't want to try again. She wasn't you and nobody else would be, either."

She opened her handbag and took out a tissue, carefully wiped her eyes. "Do you think we'd have worked, Patrick?"

I shrugged. "Hard to say, Mary. Those few weeks with you were utterly magical. I've never been so happy since, I know that. Who can say if teenage magic lasts?"

She smiled. "Maybe it was better that way? At least we've both got magical memories that didn't get messed up by reality!"

We stayed silent for a moment, just looking at each other. Those weeks flashed before me. The enchantment of that evening we met at the weekly dances in the local hall, the blood-boiling moment of the first kiss under the trees in the park, the pride as I watched her compete in the county schools athletic championships and cheered her to victory in the sprints. Then the pain as she walked away, unable to explain why. Somehow I know she was reliving those same moments.

"Can we have the odd coffee in a restaurant without bursting into tears, do you think?" she asked.

"I'd like that," I said. I took my card out of one pocket and handed it over. "Call me," I said. "Will your husband object?"

I saw the pain in her eyes. "We've been separate people for some years now. He won't care."

Just briefly, I touched her hand and felt some of the old electricity. "We'd better attend to our grandparenting duties."

She nodded and smiled. "I'll call you," she said and walked away.

I found Jason and we walked down the corridor. I felt like I could conquer worlds.

The Governor and the Old Lag
(The second story in the Park Bench series

The middle-aged man was sitting on the park bench in the sun, watching the kids playing cricket. He was drowsy, remembering the days long ago when he played with that same blissful freedom of not knowing how ugly the world could be.

A shadow fell across him and he looked up.

"Mind if I sit down?" said the intruder. He was tall, skinny in that wiry way that could never put on weight however much he consumed. His hair was cropped short, light brown at the top, graying at the sides.

The seated man shivered with the cold memories of the previous fifteen years just passed when he rarely saw the sun and his world was filled with the clangour of steel bars closing and men weeping and shouting their horrors at night.

"Governor Jackson?" he whispered, his throat tightening.

"How are you doing, Wilkins?" the man said. "Enjoying freedom?"

Wilkins was trembling. "I just got out as you know, Governor. Why are you here?"

"Wilkins, Wilkins, a good prison governor should care for the welfare of those just released. I'm just doing my duty and checking on your health." His tone was light, amused, but the other man had heard this tone before, usually before handing out a sentence of solitary confinement for a few days or more for some minor offence.

Wilkins tried to control his breathing.

"I'm doing fine, sir. I'm staying at the hostel and I'm reporting to my parole officer on time. I have a job gardening for the local hotel."

"Ah, yes, of course, you ran a little gardening business before, didn't you?"

"Yes, sir, I did."

"That was before you and you gang stole fifteen million from the armoured car and killed one of the guards in the process."

Wilkins felt his throat go dry.

"You know it was Hendry who killed that guard, sir. They proved that completely in the trial."

"And that's why you only got twenty years," said Jackson. "And they never found Hendry, did they? Nor the other one in your gang, that Beeston fellow."

"No sir, they vanished. I've always thought they took the money and ran overseas, probably South America."

Wilkins knew something terrible was going on. Fifteen years in prison tightened up a man's sense of danger.

"You got out early for good behaviour, didn't you?" said Jackson.

"You know I did, sir. You were on the parole board."

"Ah yes, so I was. Which means it wouldn't take much to throw you right back in, would it?"

By now, Wilkins was shaking with fear like a man caught outside in an ice storm.

"They never found the money, of course," said Jackson.

"I said, sir, I'm certain the other two ran off with it."

"Well, you see, Wilkins, there's a good reason to say you're lying. We talked to Hendry's wife, she's back here, never went with Hendry, she ran off to Australia because he was a violent bastard. She said she knows he never saw any money and she said Hendry told her you'd hidden it for when you got out."

Wilkins let out a sob of fear and shifted away from the other man so hard he fell off the bench. He stayed sitting on the grass, gasping in loud painful breaths.

"I didn't, sir! I don't know what happened to the money! I swear it, I waited a few days like we'd agreed before going to see Hendry and get my share, but he'd gone."

"You're lying, Wilkins. You've been lying all the time, all the years you were inside, pleading innocence, you know where the money is. Now you can tell me, or I promise you, you'll be back inside by the weekend."

"Sir, I beg you, please believe me. If I knew where it was, I'd have got it by now, but I don't."

Jackson stood up, looking down at the weeping man on the grass.

"You might as well resign from the job, Wilkins. I'll report to the Board that you've been seen drunk in the town and they'll be coming for you."

He turned and walked away toward a black Holden Commodore parked a few yards away..

"Did you get all that?" he asked as he opened the car door.

"Damn right," said the man at the wheel.

"Did you believe him?" Jackson undid his shirt and pulled away the microphone and wire.

"Not a chance. I'll pick him up tonight at the hostel and I'll make him talk."

"Like you did to Beeston?"

"Yeah, like I did to Beeston, but he was a tougher nut than that little twerp over there. I took three fingers off him before I decided he was telling the truth. I bet Wilkins will be babbling after one."

"And then you shot him?"

"And threw him in the river weighed down with scrap iron," said Hendry.

"So you're certain that Wilkins has the stuff?"

"Nobody left," said Hendry.

"And I'll get my share when?"

"You'll get the two million as soon as I find out where Wilkins hid it," said the man at the wheel.

"Call me then," said the Prison Governor and climbed out of the car.

Memories, Why?

I have often wondered why some moments become engraved permanently in one's memories. It's a common phenomenon with moments like the death of Kennedy, the first lunar landing or the first news of the death of a parent. But why the utterly ordinary? It's even understandable why I should retain the two-year old's memory of standing on the beach in Haifa Bay, my feet burning in the hot sand. But why the memory of seeing a perfectly ordinary man in a greatcoat walking along the pavement on the other side of the road in Prestwich, Manchester, when I was perhaps five? Why the memory of a teacher from infant school telling us a story about Winnie the Pooh, why that story, not any other? The clearest memories I have seem to be of that era over sixty years ago, but not the great moments, just the inconsequential ones.

I can vaguely recall seeing the headlines of the death of King George VI, I can partially remember the gathering of neighbours at the house of a rich family who actually had a television to watch the Coronation of Queen Elizabeth, but for some reason, my clearest memory of that day was drinking a small glass of beer, my first ever taste of alcohol.

Memories, Why?

Another vivid memory of that time is the one of my class teacher, Mr Panther, coming into the classroom with a package containing the souvenir propelling pencils of the Coronation, waving the package above his head in triumph to roars of applause from the thirty or so 11-year olds in the classroom. I remember the tweed jacket he wore, the wiry haircut, the thin face and wide smile. Moments later, he was followed by a more senior kid wheeling in the cartons of the souvenir mugs but I really cannot remember that particular scene. But oddly, I **can** remember clearly how the mugs looked, the white earthenware plain shape with the ornate red and white picture of the young Princess Elizabeth (as we still called her) smiling at us with that serene look of the Empress of Almost All The World.

I took mine home and used it to stand my pens and pencils in on the small table in my room where I did my homework. I don't remember the room all that clearly, or the table, but the mug with its pencils and pens stands out clearly in my mind.

I used to build flying models of aeroplanes as a kid, too. I don't remember most of them, though I do know that I built a Focke-Wulfe 110 complete with Luftwaffe insignia and I'm a little surprised now in retrospect that such a model was even sold in those bleak, rationed, post war years where every city still had its bomb sites as brittle memories of a barely won war that only ended seven years before.

The one event I remember as clearly as I remember Mr Panther coming in with the pencils, as clearly as I recall that man in his military greatcoat, was the moment when I first flew my balsa-wood model of a Spitfire. I wound up the rubber band-driven propeller, put the Spitfire gently on the road and let the propeller go. To my utter joy, it took off in a straight line, climbed to perhaps fifty feet and glided to a perfect landing half way down the road.

I'm quite sure I have never experienced such pure, uninhibited delight in my whole life since that moment of seeing my Spitfire fly. I hope I never lose that memory.

Of course, I remember my first kiss. Who doesn't? It was at a party in Chester, I had taken the train down from Manchester with my friend David to go to a party thrown by a girl I had met briefly on a train. I didn't even know the girl I kissed, it was that sort of party, a game of some sort. But what I remember most is the moment when we were playing some sort of detective question-and-answer game and I successfully identified the "killer." Why that memory as clear as the memory of my first kiss at fourteen?

There are so many occasions I *should* remember. Going up for my Bachelor's degree on Convocation Day at Birmingham University is a complete blank. The same with going up some years later for my Master's degree in Canada. But doing the Twist at a university dance with the lovely Wendy – clear as a bell. An ordinary coffee in the refectory with another friend – sharp and clear. I even remember what we talked about, nothing world-shaking!

I don't remember my first solo in a glider, nor my first flight as an instructor, not even sending a pupil off on his (her?) first solo, all of which are surely memorable moments, but I clearly remember perfectly uneventful flights when I took off, flew the circuit and landed.

Why these and not the surely critical events?

It beats me.

Killer Kids
(The third story in the Park Bench series)

They couldn't have been more than thirteen, sitting on the bench by the football field, watching the school team practice.

"So why have you come to me?" said Bailey Parkes. He unwrapped a sandwich from his backpack, examined it carefully then bit into it, chewing slowly as if savouring every moment.

"They told me you were the kid who could do this," Robin Caldwell said.

"Who told you?"

Robin shook his head. "Not telling you."

"Probably wise," said Bailey with a wide grin and took another bite of his sandwich.

Robin caught a whiff of roast beef and pickles and salivated a little, a longing look directed at the sandwich.

Bailey caught it. "No lunch?"

"They never do a lunch for me. She says she doesn't have the time."

"And they don't give you money for lunch at the canteen?"

"I think it interferes with their booze and cigarettes spending."

"That bad, huh?"

Robin wiped a tear from his eye and took a deep breath. "The house stinks of cigarette smoke and there's sometimes ash on the food. She cooks with a cigarette hanging from her mouth. He's the same, they both smoke during meals."

"And they drink?" Bailey looked at the packet of sandwiches in his backpack and decided not to take another one just yet.

"I think she starts after I've left for school, 'cos she's already far gone when I get home. He starts as soon as he gets home, she drinks sherry, he drinks vodka. That's when I get scared, 'cos if anything happens, they'll manage to blame me for it and I cop a beating."

"That's pretty rough. But what will you do when they're gone?"

"It couldn't get any worse. I imagine I'll get put in foster care, even an orphanage, but at least I'll get fed properly, I won't have cigarette ash on my food and I won't cop a beating because she spilt the milk during the day or he knocked the telephone off its stand when he was drunk."

"Well, shit, eh?" said Bailey. "I think you were right to come to me. But it'll cost you two hundred dollars. Can you raise that?"

"You know Jenny Carter in grade 8? Her dad runs that pram shop near the bank and I work there at weekends cleaning prams and general sweeping up. I've saved fifty and I'll give you that and I'll have to pay the rest over time. Will that be okay?"

"How much do you get?"

"Usually about twenty dollars for the weekend."

"Okay, we'll go with that, fifty now and then ten weeks of $20. That's pretty generous of me, really."

"That's two hundred and fifty."

"Finance charges."

Robin took a deep breath. "All right, I agree. How will you do it?"

"Easy. You know those paper suits you see in the cop shows when the pathologists come to the murder scene? That makes sure they don't contaminate the scene. I've got a few of those. I'll come in during the afternoon when she's nicely pissed, she'll probably be asleep. Perfect for cutting her throat. Then I'll just stay quiet until your father gets home, he won't be expecting anything, I'll wait for the best moment and do the same to him. Then I'll get out, wrap up the suit in a garbage bag and burn it when I get home. I won't leave a trace."

Robin was breathing hard. "What will I be doing?"

"We'll arrange this for tennis practice evening this Thursday, you join in, that will keep you here till after six. Then you go home and call the cops as soon as you get in."

"But what if somebody sees you?" Tension was making Robin's voice harsh.

"No chance. You're on the Macksfield Road, only three houses in two kilometres. I'll walk round the other places in the fields and come in from the back of the house and get back in the same way."

Robin was silent for nearly two minutes. "You're sure about this?"

Bailey grinned. "Do you know how many of these things I've done?"

"No, I don't."

"And I'm not going to tell you. But I will tell you I do it differently each time, so the cops don't get any clues from what they call the *"Modus Operandi,"* the way of doing it. If I use a knife, it then gets thrown into the lake, though it can't have any finger prints on it. I used a gun once, I was able to get a .22 pistol and that went in the lake as well."

Robin took a deep breath. "Okay, I'll bring the money in tomorrow."

"Here's what you do," said Bailey. "Put on gloves, wipe each note with a damp cloth, take an envelope from the middle of the pack, still wearing the gloves and put the notes inside. Don't lick the envelope, just close the envelope without sealing it. That'll make sure you leave no fingerprints or DNA to connect you to me. Tomorrow morning, put the envelope in an exercise book and hand that to me. Later, I'll give it back to you after I've wiped the cover clean of my fingerprints. Is that all clear?"

Robin nodded, his face a little pale.

Bailey smiled. "It's fool proof," he said. "Nobody can connect us and if anyone has seen us talking today, we were just watching the football practice like a dozen or more kids are doing."

He waved an arm round the scene and he was correct, a number of students were sitting around watching the practice session. He reached into his backpack and extracted the packet of sandwiches, handing it to Robin.

"Here," he said. "Thanks for the business."

The Time of the Snakes

This was always the time he loved most, soon after sun-up with no wind, the heat of summer not yet biting and no noise but birdsong, cicada calls and occasional frogs down by the lily-pond. He strolled around the garden, coffee mug in hand, occasionally bending to pull out a fire-weed or dandelion and noting the occasional small shoot of a lantana sprouting that would get the attention of the weedkiller after breakfast.

As he stood up from pulling out a dandelion, he shivered. A cold breeze wafted by him and then the sun seemed to fade, and with it the light.

"What the hell?" he muttered as it became darker and darker. He could only make out the shape of the house because the night-lights in the kitchen and corridor had responded to the gloom and were gently casting a small glow through the windows. Becoming increasingly worried, he began to move to the small patio outside the kitchen but stopped short.

Four grass snakes stood in his path. They reared up and glared at him, their cold, beady eyes reflecting hatred. Each was perhaps two metres long, large for such snakes, but they weren't dangerous. He hated snakes. He stared back at them, feeling small shivers begin to run down his back. At the precise same moment, the snakes returned to lying prone and they moved aside a metre or two. He started walking carefully to the patio again, but something made him look to his rear.

Two large diamond-backed pythons were rearing up, not two metres from him and they gave him the same cold stare as the smaller snakes had done. Shivering now, he kept enough clear thinking to realise the cicadas and the frogs were silent. There was not a sound to be heard.

Desperately trying to stay calm, he reached the patio and opened the door, slid inside and slammed the door shut. By now it was as dark as night and he switched on the lights. Realising how frightened he was, he gasped with relief when the lights came on. He picked up the telephone, not sure who to call, but somebody, *anybody* to see if this weird darkness was everywhere. But the phone was dead.

He heard a sound of tapping on the glass panes of his kitchen door. Hardly breathing, he moved the curtain aside and froze. The four grass snakes were tapping their noses against the glass and behind them he could just make out the two pythons, again reared up and again staring at him. He dropped the curtain again and walked into his lounge room.

The same tapping was coming from the door onto the deck. The curtain was open and already he could see three more snakes tapping their noses against the glass. Almost hypnotised, he stared at them, realising these were not harmless grass snakes. These were Browns, deadly as anything in the country. He was having trouble breathing.

It was getting colder. He found a sweater in the bedroom next to the lounge. The heaters wouldn't come on.

The tapping was louder and becoming concerted. Tap.... Tap.... Tap..... Not just on the door to the deck and the door to the patio but on all the windows. He jumped to the window looking out to the garden to close the curtain. He was staring at a massive python that glared back at him, eye-to-eye.

A small snake crawled across the carpet without looking at him. He saw a whole number of them lying against the wall. In utter panic, he raced for the front door, snatched the car keys off the hook, flung open the door, trying not to think of the lethal Browns and ran for the car. Fumbling in terrifying clumsiness to open the car door, he was slammed against the side of the vehicle by a blow in his back, making him drop the keys.

He only had time to see the thick torso of another python that must have been wider than he was when he felt the pain of the bite on his ankle. His strength faded and he sank to ground, looking at the fangs of a Brown as it stared back at him.

"Gotcha," said the snake as his eyes closed for the last time.

Life

"Well, well, well," said Frank Burton in delight and surprise, and died.

"I'm sorry," said the doctor, looking down at the bed. "He's gone."

"Indeed I have," said Frank Burton, but of course, nobody heard him, not that he knew of at the time, anyway. He watched as his wife broke into tears, and decided she was a better actress than he had ever realized.

"She's only thinking about the money I've left her," he said, finding it quite unremarkable that he could read Marlene's thoughts as clearly as if she were speaking aloud. "The old bitch!" he grinned to himself, still a little shaken and delighted with the vision he had seen as death came to him.

He looked at the doctor's impersonal face above him, then again at his wife's improbable weeping. "Now what happens when I sit up?" he said aloud. "Do they scream and holler and run for the door? Or maybe they don't notice?"

He exercised muscles as he had always done to sit up from a recumbent position. The task was a lot easier that it had been for many years. On the high hospital bed, he was now looking at his wife from the same level, but neither she nor the doctor seemed to have noticed.

"Interesting," said Frank Burton and got off the bed, looking down at his own body. "It looks smaller than I remember it."

The doctor folded up his stethoscope and placed it in a pocket of his white coat. He walked out of the room, and Marlene immediately stopped snuffling.

"You old bastard," she grated. "You'd better have left me something or I'll..." She stopped, and Frank saw the confusion in her mind.

"Silly old sausage," he laughed. "You'll be okay, though for the life of me, I wonder why I left it all to you..." He stopped, amused at his own choice of words, and also because Marlene seemed to advancing threateningly on him.

"Whoops!" he said, beginning to move out of the way, but he was too late. Automatically flinching at her furious face only inches away from his, he closed his eyes. But when he opened them a second later, she had walked through him, and was out the door. He grinned at himself.

"Silly bastard," he said. "You're dead! There's nothing she can do to you anymore."

He reflected on the sudden, beautiful image he had seen as he died. The light had turned gold, and he had experienced a wave of such wonder and love that he had felt his body jerk. All the sickness he had been feeling for so long had vanished, like a sudden cool breeze blowing away the humid rotten air of a jungle where something had died. His pounding headache had calmed, and he had felt as purely healthy and energetic as a teenager. There had been something else.... some other place.... The image had gone, but the happiness had remained within him. *No matter,* he thought. *It's where I'm going, eventually.*

"Actually, this is rather weird," he said, then looked around and raised his voice. "I'm dead," he called loudly. "What am I doing still here in the hospital? What happened to the ascension to heaven, or whatever?"

Nobody answered. He tried again.

"OYE!" he yelled with lungs that had recovered the power of sixty years ago. Two doctors walking by the ward talking quietly didn't miss a step. They didn't look into the ward, nor did they stop talking.

"Well, that's obviously not going to work," said Frank. "I suppose I should be frightened about this..." He stopped, realizing that fear was simply not present anywhere in his mind. It was an astounding sensation. With pulse-thundering clarity, he saw how he had been a little afraid, or a lot afraid almost all his life. First, he had been afraid of his father. The menace emanating from that silent man had always been a presence. Frank recalled how, if he stayed within his father's reach for more than a few minutes, there would be an explosion of violence, a huge hand slamming into his face and a roar of rage. "What do you mean by...?" was always the opening blast.

Later, it had been at school. Frank had been bright, despite the screaming insistence of his father that he was a fool, a nothing, stupid.... And in a school such as he had attended, being bright was a crime among his fellows. Being top of the class was an invitation to a beating.

Even later, fear had come from dealing with bosses, banks, the IRS... Frank had learned to hide it, to show a strong face to the world, to be successful, even wealthy. But the fear had remained as a tiny companion to every living day.

When he married, later than most men, near the end of his thirties, there had been a new source. Her biting tongue and rabid selfishness had meant that Frank could never, ever do the right thing. Just how two children had come along was a source of mystification to Frank. He could never be certain that he was the father, but didn't really want to find out. He had loved the two girls, and they had responded to him far more than to their mother, who had never forgiven them for that crime. By the time the girls had left to their own lives, Frank was nearly sixty, and leaving Marlene was just too complicated. He contented himself with adding a study to the house, and retreating there for almost all his time at home.

But now, he felt no fear. It was an astonishing feeling, as if he had spent years in a gloomy, stuffy room, and had just walked out into a spring morning in Vermont.

He looked back at his body on the bed. It was no more distressing than looking at a suit of clothes he had just taken off to have a shower.

"I wonder..." he muttered, and looked down at himself. He saw the same view he had seen for his whole life, modified as time had done what time does. At seventy, his body racked with disease, thin as a broom stick and shoulders hunched to protect against the agonies of the perpetual cough, he had not looked down at himself for some years. Now he did, and decided it was an ugly view, unimproved by the hideous hospital gown he wore.

"But there isn't a body," he told himself. "So this horrible little thing isn't me. It's what I'm used to, so it's what I've made..." He stopped as he realized the truth of his words. He had made it. So he could unmake it, or remake it. He concentrated. He looked again.

He was six foot tall, dressed in well-tailored slacks and a blue sweater. The breadth of his shoulders was deeply satisfying, as was the flat line of his stomach.

"Nice," he said, and grinned. He turned to the mirror on the wall and studied the image. Thin face, dark red hair, wide mouth. "Now, am I creating that image in the mirror as well, or am I actually seeing a reflection?" he mused. "Has to be my own efforts," he decided. "There's nothing to reflect, after all." He walked out of the room with an energetic stride.

"This death thing is alright," he said with a laugh to himself. "I wish I'd thought of it sooner. Now, let's get out of here and see what fun I can get up to. I have a feeling I'm supposed to do something before the next stage."

In no great haste he ambled along the ward, quite unnoticed by medical staff and visitors. On impulse, he turned into the room of a man he'd talked to briefly when they sat next to each other in wheelchairs, waiting to be X-rayed. The man lying on the bed looked asleep but his eyes opened as Frank looked at the nameplate above the bed. Brad Fielding, it said.

Frank stood still by Brad's shoulders.

"G'day, Brad," he said, more to feel normal than with any thought that the sick man would hear him. The result was unexpected. Brad smiled gently.

"Now what on Earth did I just hear?" he said softly.

Frank was shaken. "Did you hear me, Brad?" he asked, startled.

"This is weird," said Brad, the smile still on his face.

"Brad, can you hear me?" said Frank once more.

45

But there was no further reaction from the man on the bed. Frank remained standing for a few more moments, his mind in a whirl then decided to move along and see what other reactions he might get. His own thoughts brought him to a halt outside Brad's door.

"What the hell is going on?" he said out loud. "I'm supposed to be dead. I *know* I'm dead. Why am I here? Why haven't I gone somewhere, been greeted by an angel, or whatever is supposed to happen?"

Three young people were walking past him and one, a girl in her twenties, smiled at him and said, "It'll all get clear soon, Frank."

WHAT? Frank stared at her retreating back as she continued along the corridor, engaged in a lively three-way conversation with her companions. Frank raced after her, stopped in front of her and kept walking backwards, staring at the girl.

"What did you say to me?" he demanded.

She seemed not to have heard him, but looked at the man on her right as he was telling some story.

"Stop!" pleaded Frank and put his hand on her shoulders. She kept on moving, walked right through him and continued her conversation.

Baffled, Frank let her pass and stared at her retreating back. *She had spoken to him, looked into his face, she must have known what she was doing,* he told himself.

His attention was attracted to the door he had left when he had stopped by Brad's room. Brad was standing outside the room, looking cheerful. Frank walked back and looked at him and Brad looked back.

"You can see me?" asked Frank.

"See you? Of course I can see you, why shouldn't I?"

"You didn't when I was in your room a few minutes ago."

Brad looked puzzled.

"I heard something!" he said. "Somebody spoke to me! But there was nobody there."

"I was there. I spoke to you."

Brad looked at him and then smiled with great delight. "I'm dead, aren't I? I should have realised! I feel great! But I've been feeling like shit for months."

"That's what seems to happen," said Frank. "But nothing else. Aren't we supposed to go somewhere?"

A look of great wonder came over Brad's face and his eyes glowed.

"We are," he said and vanished.

What is going on? Why can't I go wherever he just went? I thought we discovered everything when we die. Feeling depressed and angry, he walked on and saw two people leaving another room, both greatly distressed, the young woman was weeping while the man, perhaps her husband kept his arm round her shoulder, tears rolling down his own cheeks.

Sensing the need, Frank walked into the room. A small child was lying on the bed, barely making a shape under the blanket, so thin and frail was he. His face was chalk white.

"Oh you poor kid," said Frank.

The little boy looked at him. "Hi," he said and managed a small smile.

Shock ran through Frank. "You can see me?" he said.

"Yup!" said the boy. "But I bet nobody else can."

Astonished, Frank took a seat next to the bed. "Why not?" he asked.

"Because you're dead," said the boy. "I'll be dead soon." As he spoke, tears began running down the boy's face. "It's not fair!" he sobbed.

"No, it's not. But I can tell you, something wonderful happens. I've just seen it, I just saw my old friend die and he was so happy as he went."

The boy took a deep breath. "Then why haven't you gone?" he said.

The logic of children! Frank almost laughed, remembering how well he had always got on with kids, somehow finding a bond that gained their trust.

"I don't know," he replied. "But I think there's a reason, maybe I have to do something first."

"Yes, that's it," said the child. "You know what? You've made me feel a lot better about this. I think I'll go now."

He closed his eyes and Frank knew that the child had died, peacefully and without pain. He sat and watched the child lie there with a small smile on his face. Without warning, the boy sat up, leaving the body behind, grinned cheerfully and said, "Hey!" Then he vanished.

"He's right, of course," said a voice from the doorway.

Startled, Frank turned and saw a young man dressed in the saffron robes of a Buddhist monk.

"No, I'm not dead," said the young man.

"But you can see me?"

"Perks of the trade," said the monk with a smile.

"But what about the woman who spoke to me before? She couldn't see me or hear me when she spoke."

"She didn't speak. It was your spirit guide who spoke to you. Your mind just made it seem that she had."

"I have no idea what's going on," said Frank. "Why am I still here?"

"Your choice."

"Mine?"

"Yours. Remember what you thought just now, about how you and kids have always got on so well? You need to stick around, go and talk to all the sick kids, show them there's nothing to be afraid of and tell them they'll be back soon."

"They will?"

"They will. So will you, in a few decades. That's how it works."

"Reincarnation?" Frank was delighted. Somehow he had always believed in that idea.

"Indeed," said the monk. "My lot are the only ones that really know about that. I've been back thirty times and I can remember them all."

Frank felt all his doubts, all his anxieties, all the anger fade. He stood up. He had a wonderful job to do and he didn't care how long it took. He walked out of the room in search of the next child that needed comforting as he or she faced death.

Farinelli

When Alex Castle sang in the junior school choir, he had a beautiful voice. It was the classic boy's soprano, cold, pure, perfect, the voice of the sexless angel that could send shivers down the listener's back.

Once, a music teacher at his school made a joke among his friends that the boy should be castrated to preserve the voice of Farinelli, the greatest countertenor in history. Nobody thought it funny and he never repeated the joke.

But as Alex turned twelve, as his friends developed pimples and hair on various body parts, their voices trembled and broke, sometimes squeaking and sometimes croaking before settling into the sounds of young men, Alex didn't get the memo.

Most of the right things happened, though. His shoulders expanded, he found he needed to shave with increasing frequency and he found himself becoming breathless at the sight of the girls in the class as they developed bumps and curves that had not been there the previous year.

But his voice didn't change, not when he sang, anyway, though in normal speech he had a young man's voice, a pleasant tenor, in fact. But his singing voice had developed into a mature range, with a new colour and tone of great depth and strength. He stopped singing in the school choir though, because the soprano and alto parts were filled by the girls and there just was not room for a muscular, handsome young man singing in the high registers.

His classmates gave him hell in the cruel way that young people adopt so easily. They joked about his high voice, minced around like pseudo chorus girls, called him a pooftah and they never let him forget it, even though he didn't sing at school.

Much of the abuse he silenced by becoming a fine rugby player, demonstrating a ferocious, fearless style of play that resulted in many opposing players being helped off the field. And when one pair of bullies attacked him after school, he beat them both senseless. That stopped the pooftah calls.

Anyway, the girls liked him and that ended any further difficulties. He took the school beauty to the end of year dance and the whole school watched as she danced most of the evening with her head on his shoulder.

"You do seem to fit there very well," murmured Alex, conscious of how his arm encased her slender waist and her perfume drifted up to his nose.

She chuckled. "I'm not sure how this happened, Alex, but I like it."

"Me too."

"Some of the girls at school said they'd heard from some of the boys that you were gay."

"And?"

"They're talking crap. You're deliciously male, Alex!"

"Thank 'ee, Ma'am!" he said. "I think you've killed that nonsense off!"

"I should damn well think so. Now, I think we should go outside for a snog in the bushes."

They walked out, hand in hand, Alex very conscious of the envious stares he was getting from some of his one-time tormentors.

One day, on the advice of his music teacher who was teaching him the piano, Alex went to a concert in the town hall and afterwards talked to one of the choir who directed him to the concert master, one Charles Alderton.

"I'm a countertenor," said Alex. "Can you use one?"

"Good God, yes! Countertenors are very hard to find. Come backstage, let's hear you."

Ten minutes later, Charles was staring at Alex in a mixture of astonishment and delight.

"We're doing a concert of Vivaldi, Handel and Bach next month," he said. "I want you to sing a couple of parts."

The scholarship offer from the Conservatorium came just two months after the concert.

* * *

The standing ovation at the Sydney Opera House after a recital of Baroque music and songs for Countertenor led to much comment in the musical world and general consensus that this was the new Farinelli, the greatest Countertenor in history. Within another year, Alex was much in demand and was performing all over the world. Nobody ever called him a pooftah again.

Little-Known Episodes in Australian History

Australian history is full of well-worn anecdotes, ranging from ancient stories of the Dream Time through to modern tales of boring stuff, like Captain Cook's landing, the founding of Parramatta and some bloke called John Kerr who nearly messed up the whole bloody thing.

Less is known about some episodes which, while not in the history books, had a massive impact on the social life and culture of Australia. One of these is the story of the ancient Clan von Schnitzelgruber from the small hamlet of Loch Ochaye in northern Scotland. Although the von Schnitzelgrubers had a long and glorious history in Scotland, our story begins in 1845 when the patriarch of the clan, Heinrich von Schnitzelgruber left Ochaye to move to Australia. Heinrich von Schnitzelgruber was a haggis-farmer when he travelled with his wife Zelda and they set up a small property in the Snowy Mountains. They had brought with them five pairs of breeding haggises.

Haggises thrived and he found a ready market among the Scottish nobility who had long been deprived of the ancient Scottish sport of Haggis-hunting. The von Schnitzelgruber haggises were renowned for their speed and nimbleness that they soon became uncatchable to the footbound hunters, following the ancient Scottish tradition of being unable to ride a horse.

VON SCHNITZELGRUBER (TRIAL 1)

But the problem that soon arose was that the original Scottish haggises lived in the highlands and lived their lives on the steep slopes, following the sun from east to west and eating the fresh grass. Evolution had caused them to have longer right legs than left in order to move easily on the slopes. But in the southern hemisphere, the Coriolis Effect somehow made the haggises graze from west to east, and that meant they were unable to stand upright and always fell down the mountains. The von Schnitzelgruber haggises were successfully bred with left legs longer than the right and so thrived.

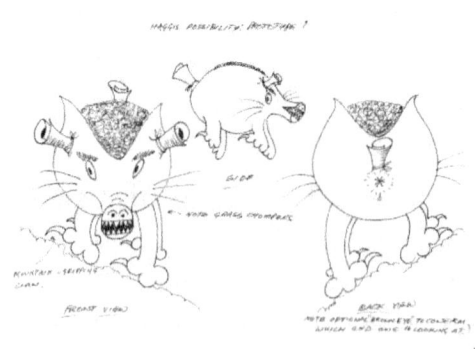

Heinrich and Zelda had two boys, Alphonse and Percy and they saw the market opportunity to breed haggis hounds that were skilled in hunting the haggises through any conditions. These were bred with right legs longer than the left and were trained to hunt from the opposite direction of the haggis grazing patterns and so made the haggises turn and run, immediately falling down the mountain where they could be collected by the Scottish manservants. However, as haggis breeding became wider spread with haggises being bred mainly as a food source, haggis farms appeared in western NSW in the flat lands and within a few generations, the "Level Haggis" evolved with equi-length legs. This resulted in time in the national sport of haggis hound trials being developed.

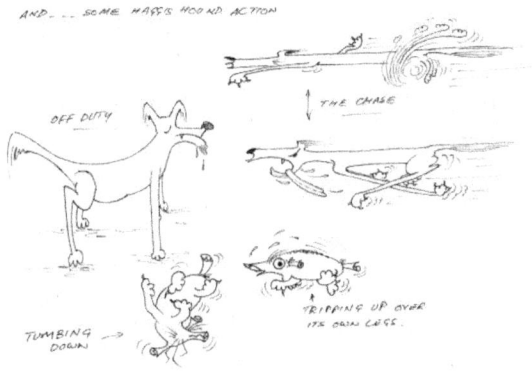

Evolution of the tree-climbing haggis

After two seasons of heavy flooding in western NSW, many of the equi-length haggises took to climbing trees and breeding in nests they constructed. This resulted in the phenomenon of "Drop-Haggises" as young haggises jumped on passing people, inflicting serious scratches and other injuries. A program of culling the tree-climbing version was successful and this danger passed.

Evolution of the sea-going haggis

Many roaming flocks of escaped haggises that left the breeding farms after the floods reached the south-eastern coast of Victoria. They swam across the Tasman and invaded NZ, becoming a major problem, competing with the sheep for grass. With no natural predator, they quickly became a plague until Saint Hieronymus von Schnitzelgruber sailed over to NZ and after six weeks of prayer and the sacred haggis-banning rites which involved playing the Bach Toccata and Fugue on the bagpipes while walking up the Franz Joseph Glacier in his tartan underpants, string vest and white wing collar and black bow tie, he was successful. Within days of performing this rite every 6am, noon and 5pm, all traces of the NZ haggis had disappeared. To this day, New Zealand sheep-farmers celebrate Haggis-Banning Day, or in Kiwi, "Huggus-Bunning Day" with a re-enactment of the Saint Hieronymus rites on Mount Cook.

Evolution of haggis-hound trials as a national sport

Haggises developed the art of protection of the Queen Haggis by circling round her, thus requiring the Gliding Hound to be developed. Alphonse became famous for his training techniques in which the specially-bred Gliding Hound grew a sizeable membrane between the legs on each side and by extending them could glide significant distances, often as much as thirty metres. Haggis hound trials thus became a test of the hound's ability to leap from outside the pack of haggises and glide a complex path to the Queen Haggis, separating her out from the guarding haggises and drive her into the fenced enclosure. *Aficionados* of the sport claimed that the *"glisser à droit"* demonstrated the true technique, while the *"glisser à gauche"* was by far the least skilful and less attractive approach and invariably scored worse with the judges.

However, the sport was badly damaged by the great Fart Propulsion Scandal of 1969. At the Haggis Hound Grand Finals in Windsor, the massive spectator crowd was astounded when the lead hound belonging to Perseus von Schnitzlegruber, a minor breeder of hounds and a distant relative of the main line of the von Schnitzelgruber Clan

Flying haggis hounds after the queen Haggis

was seen to soar several hundred feet into the air before arrowing down almost vertically onto the Queen Haggis surrounded by her protective guard of soldier haggises.

The collision caused the instant death of both Queen and hound, leaving a massive pile of guts, bone and blood on the grass. Competition referees were called immediately and delicately poked their way through the ugly mess. After a few minutes, one of them called out a discovery of something unusual, a small, metallic object, roughly spherical in shape but with a large hole on one side and a nozzle opposite the hole, and two straps.

Later forensic examination assisted by aeronautical engineers decided that the device was strapped over the anus of the haggis hound with the hole over the anal exit and the nozzle pointing backwards. A fart from the hound caused an automatic compression of the thick air and a spark ignited the compressed gas which then blew out the nozzle providing a significant fart-assisted jet stream. Further post mortem examination of the hound revealed that it had been fed a meal of Coco-Pops just before the event and this had generated major flatulence leading to several fart-assisted reheat jet pulses that had lifted the hound to an altitude of well over two hundred metres.

A tribunal of the Stewards of the Haggis Hound Trials Association held that Perseus von Schnitzlegruber was guilty of unlawfully applying engineering assistance to his hounds. He was banned for life from the sport and stripped of the trophy he had won in 1965.

The Children of Heinrich von Schnitzelgruber

Percy von Schnitzelgruber went into Kangaroo training to solve the problems of transport across the Nullarbor. He was the primary designer of the Nullarbor Stage Coach and trained the Big Red Fliers to leap in pairs and in succession in rubberised harnesses to eliminate whip-lash for the passengers.

Percy's son was Ned von Schnitzelgruber who became an outlaw, robbing the Nullarbor Coaches. Notorious for

wearing a coal scuttle on his head, he was known as "Wrong Way Schnitzelgruber" for his propensity for racing off after a robbery, going the wrong way and right into the patrolling local police. He only escaped because the cops tended to shit their drawers with laughter at the sight, allowing him to run away from them. He was eventually apprehended by a particularly humourless cop, Senior Sergeant Audrey Li Wong, a Bolivian immigrant outside Roo Dropping, New South Wales. He was sentenced to spend five years listening to speeches in the State Upper House and although he survived this brutal punishment, he lived the rest of his life in an insane asylum, muttering, "He's gone troppo, Mr Speaker," and similar incomprehensible phrases.

Eurydice von Schnitzelgruber

Eurydice von Schnitzelgruber was the daughter of Alphonse and the renowned Clan beauty. But she was also a poet of international renown. These are some samples of her works.

EURIDYCE VON S. + GAWPERS.

Meditations on a Hunkenscheisenhauser

"My Love is like a royal blue Hunkenscheisenhauser.
It glows like perriwinkels in a stream of porridge.
Whoflungdung and whatchermercallit.
Carry on, Admiral."

Memories, Why?

Reflections on an Aromatic Marsupial

"Oh Pooh!
It stinks!
Who pooped here?
Why, a Koala Bear!
A very ancient Koala Bear.
Little Bastard.
Carry on, General."

Ariadne's Protest

"Don't Come The Raw Prawn with me,
Mate.
My dad's a General
Wallabies live in my bedroom
And cane toads
So bloody watch it.
Carry on, Colonel."

Ode to Tucker

"Abalone, prawns and scallops
Aussie seafood tucker
Drink till we're legless
And rat-arsed.
Carry on, Corporal."

Revelations on the Homeland

"Pommies are rubbish
Can't play cricket
Never wash
Can't surf
Useless gits.
Carry on, Major."

Wotan von Schnitzelgruber

Wotan von Schnitzelgruber, a late addition to Alphonse's offspring, enlisted in the Australian Army to fight in WWI after changing his name to Hochscheisenhaus to avoid sounding like a German. His brigade was sent to France and he fought in the little-known battle of la Petite Eglise du Lac des Deux Montagnes d'Avignon where, with 25 other troops on patrol they encountered a similar German patrol in dense fog. Both sides turned and ran and both fell into their trenches, suffering several broken legs and bruises. Rescued by a later patrol of his own brigade, he was patched up and transferred to the 45th Woolloomolloo Scouts Troop where he served for three years before he was arrested for inappropriate training methods which mostly consisted of asking the boys to strip naked and cavort in front of him. After five years in Long Bay Gaol, he was released but never heard of again, though some rumours placed him as a Bishop in a remote Catholic diocese.

The family of von Schnitzelgrubers continues to this day with a continuing record of powerful influences on Australian history.

The Chicken Bowl

He had seen her even in the initial lineup, not because she was beautiful but because she looked so crabby, so miserable, and so apart from all the rest. Unlike the cheerful crowds of visitors still coming into the grounds of the University, she talked to nobody, clutching her handbag as if frightened that somebody would steal it.

"What do you think she's got in that bag?" he asked his assistant.

"God knows," said Elizabeth. "Anything from the crown jewels to her lunch, I reckon."

"I've got a very odd feeling about this," he said. "Why don't you go and check her out and see what she is bringing to the show?"

"Will do," said Elizabeth and strolled off in the direction of the long line-up of people coming in to the broadcast.

He consulted his notes and saw that his first meeting would be with a young man who had some ceramic pots to display. His table was outside the Great Hall of the University, set up in the sunshine on the hard ground of the walkway surrounding the central lawn. The meeting was an interesting and valuable session because the pots turned out to be 17th-century classics which he valued at about £2500 to the great pleasure of the young man. While he was waiting for the next interview, Elizabeth walked up to him.

"I think you should see this," she said. "She's got something interesting there."

"What is it?" he asked.

"It's a little bowl," she replied. "But there is something about it..."

"Well, okay, bring her along." He looked around for the producer, saw her watching another display and went up to her. "Judith, can I have the cameras to my table? I may have an interesting ceramic display."

"Sure," she said and waved to the cameraman at the table, pointed at his table at the cameraman nodded, understanding where to go next.

Andrew strolled back to his table and sat down to wait for the next client. As usual, a small crowd gathered around the table to see what would develop, anything from a very disappointed client to an ecstatic person who has suddenly seen lots of money in front of him or her.

Elizabeth arrived at that moment with a small woman that they had seen in the queue the company. "Andrew, this is Mrs Hopkins and she wants to show you this thing she has."

At the same moment, the cameraman arrived and took his position.

Andrew got to his feet and politely extended his hand to the woman. "Good morning, Mrs Hopkins thank you for coming to the 'Antiques Roadshow' and bringing something to show us. Would you like to take a seat?"

The women sat down still clutching her bag. Her face was hostile, the mouth turned down at the ends in what looked like a permanent expression of disapproval. Andrew felt very disconcerted but he was a professional and he played his role well.

"And so just what is it you have brought us?" he asked.

"It's a bit of pottery I got from my husband," she said. "The bastard walked out on me but I took this from his room before he could take it away."

Andrew sat back, shaken. The anger and hostility in the woman was palpable. He controlled his dismay and smiled. "Well, can I see it?"

As if about to change her mind at any moment, the woman opened the bag and took out another velvet bag tied up with a string. Slowly she unwrapped it and took out the contents. Andrew took a deep breath and tried to hide the shock. The woman put the bowl in the middle of the table and glared at him.

"How much is it worth?"

Andrew didn't reply, but gently stroked the side of the bowl with one finger. He could see his finger trembling and the shock was still sending pulses of excitement through his body. The utter beauty of the shape of the little bowl was hypnotic.

"Do you know what this is?" he said.

"I don't care what it is," she snapped. "I just want to know if it's worth anything. So, is it?"

"Mrs Hopkins, this is a widely watched television program and the cameras are on this table right now. We need to talk about this little thing so that the audience knows what's happening and understands what it is you brought to us. At the end of that I'll tell you how much it's worth."

"Well get on with it then," she demanded.

Andrew smothered his anger. "Can I ask you how you got it?"

"I told you, I got it from my husband and he owes me a hell of a lot more than this."

"Do you have a bill of sale or anything that may prove it is legally yours?"

"I don't need a bloody bill of sale," she snapped. "I took it, it's mine."

He suppressed his irritation once more. "We'll come back to that in a moment," he said. "First let me say that this is called a chicken bowl. As you can see it has a pattern of chickens around the side."

"Of course I can see that!" the woman said in irritation. "You think I'm blind, or something? It looks bloody silly, as far as I'm concerned."

"Well, you may change your mind soon," he said. "This is Chinese, it was made in the time of the emperor Shen Hua in the 15th century. Now so far, there are only nineteen known to exist in the world. You have just made it twenty. Can you tell me a little more of how your husband got it?"

He looked around the group standing round the table. The expressions on the watchers varied from disgust at the woman's behaviour and interest in what he was saying. He turned back to the woman. Her impatience was making her shift in her chair every few seconds.

"I think he got it when he was in the Navy," she said. "He said he bought it at a market somewhere in China. He never displayed it, just kept it in a drawer by his bed.

Didn't bother me, I thought it was just some crappy little bowl, but he seemed to like it, so that's why I took it."

Andrew took a deep breath.

"Now here is why you may need to prove that you own this thing legally. The last one that came onto the market was at a sale in Hong Kong a year or two ago and it fetched... $36.3 million. That's American dollars."

There was a loud concerted gasp from the audience and several of them whispered the amount to each other. Andrew watched the woman's face. She seemed frozen.

"How much is that in pounds?" she whispered.

"About twenty million," he said.

"Well that bastard isn't getting any of it," she said. "It's all mine."

"Mrs Hopkins," said Andrew. "It won't be that simple and I think you need to go to him and discuss this in a civilised fashion."

"You think I'm going to share this money with that bastard?" she shouted. "There's no way."

"You will have problems," he said. "For a start, you won't be able to sell it without proving provenance."

"Don't tell me what I can and cannot do!" she shouted. "I'll do what I bloody well like."

She waved her arms about in agitation. One hand caught the bowl and knocked it off the table. It fell to the floor and shattered into tiny pieces.

Sir John Barbarolli and Me

So I was sitting behind my market stall on a weekend as so often, thinking about life, how it worked out, sometimes playing the "what if?" game – what if parents hadn't moved from Manchester to Reading when I was fifteen, what if I had got a place at Nottingham University instead of Birmingham, what if I'd succeeded at the RAF College at Cranwell, etc., and then came the big one.

Twelve years old, I'd just finally put the last payment after two years on the violin I'd been saving for with the shop of Paul Voight on the main road going into Manchester and finding that violin lessons cost money. I didn't have any. I'd saved for two years, putting every penny I could scrounge into the savings for the violin. Parents refused, of course. Mother had no money anyway and what she got from making the odd dress for people went on cigarettes. Father simply refused out of principle

Then one day I went round to see my favourite Uncle, Jack who lived quite nearby in the same area we did, the slightly run-to-seed, once-fashionable area of Victoria Park in Rusholme. Jack had recently divorced Renée, a shocking thing in those days, the early fifties and often was glad of the company. But today, he already had company. The craggy-faced individual sitting in the armchair seemed vaguely familiar.

"John, this is my nephew, Michael," said Jack. "Mike, this is John Barbarolli. I've known him for years."

Oh my God! Of course I knew the face! The celebrated and much loved conductor of the famous Hallé Orchestra, Manchester's pride and joy. I'd been to a few school concerts in the Free Trade Hall and watched in fascination as the conductor drew the beautiful music from the musicians in front of him. I'd read every book on the orchestra I could find since I was seven, I knew where every instrument was located and this is what had started the great desire to play an instrument.

My astonishment must have shown in my face and I was speechless at first, but the great man was used to this. Finally, I was able to tell him I knew about him, the orchestra and how much I wanted to play the violin which I had just bought.

"You bought it yourself?" he asked curiously. "Your parents didn't get it for you?"

"They couldn't afford it."

"So how did you?"

I shrugged. "Paper round, running errands for people, Jack gave me ten bob for my birthday."

"And where did you buy it?"

"Paul Voight. And he gave me a case."

He nodded with a pleased smile. "We all know Paul of course. So where are you learning to play?"

"I'm not. I can't afford lessons."

"You what?" He seemed shocked.

"I can't afford lessons."

He looked at Jack. "Is this right?"

Jack nodded sadly. "My brother is not a good parent and he seems to dislike the boy. I've never known why."

"We can't not let somebody who wants to play music as badly as you do, not learn," said Barbarolli. He took a notepad from his pocket and scrawled something on it, giving me the paper. "Take this to that woman, tell her I gave it to you, you'll get your lessons."

Two years later, I was playing with the Schools Orchestra, three years after that, I got the scholarship to the London School of Music....

Except that I didn't. None of it happened. I really had saved up to buy the violin, Paul Voight really had given me the case, Uncle Jack really was an old friend of John Barbarolli, but I never met him. If parents were ever going to visit Jack when Barbarolli was there, I was prevented from going so that the meeting I just described never happened. I only discovered about Jack's friendship when I was in my twenties, talking to my elder sister who had met him. She was trying to go to Italy to become involved with the world of opera, her utter passion. Barbarolli introduced her to a family friend who gave her a job in Milan at La Scala,

I didn't get violin lessons. Eventually I gave the instrument to a little girl who seemed to have the same dreams I'd had.

What if, eh?

Memories, Why?

The Romance Writers

Ariadne de la Force (*née* Beatrice Higginbottom of Bradford) achieved her dream of becoming a famous writer when her first romantic novel, *"Rhonda Finds Happiness in Rome"* was published in 1975. It sold well and her second romantic novel, *"Matilda Finds Happiness in Munich"* was produced later in 1976. It was followed by *"Deborah Finds Happiness in Dorking"* and soon after, by *"Lavinia Finds Happiness in Liverpool"* and by this time, Ariadne de la Force was the highest-earning writer in Australia. By the time *"Zelda Finds Happiness in Zurich"* was published in 1985, more than twenty of her books had been released and all had shot to Number One on the best seller lists, particularly the New York Times Literary Supplement.

At that time, Leviticus Brown, a lecturer in literature at the University of Darwin wrote a critical article on the works of Ariadne de la Force.

"After checking through each of the books of Ariadne de la Force," he wrote, "it is glaringly obvious that all her books are identical, and that each new work was produced after using the "Global Replace" function in the word

71

processing software to change the names of the two main protagonists and places, but that was all. Beyond that, every book is word for word the same as every other book."

Mr Brown went on to comment, "This says nothing good about the ethics of the author, the ethics and literary skills of the publishers and the intelligence and analytical talents of the women who read this garbage."

A senior editor for the publishing industry and spokeswoman for the Australian Guild of Women Writers, Ms Knickerflasher Twinkletits was harshly critical of Mr Brown's article.

"If the story is brilliant, imaginative, creative and touches the soul of its women readers, then the tale can be repeated again and again and will always have the same result. Our readers don't care about repeated themes, they buy the books of Ariadne de la Force in order to experience the moving emotional sensations that she produces and learn about the exotic locations in which she places her stories. Anyway, all romance novels have the same theme. Only a man could write this criticism, because it's only men who want stories to be different and original, but everybody in the publishing industry knows that all men are beer-swilling, sports-obsessed, illiterate oafs who don't read books, which is why we don't bother producing books for the bastards."

At time of writing, Ariadne's fortieth book, *"Hortense Finds Happiness in Hawaii"* was hitting the stands with advance sales already breaking all records. She is believed to be working on another book, *"Gabrielle Finds Happiness in Gundawindi."*

After two years of intense lobbying by the Australian Guild of Women Writers, Professor Leviticus Brown was fired from his post at the University of Darwin after a committee of women professors found him guilty of anti-feminist philosophies. However, he proceeded to make an absolute fortune writing a series of erotic bondage novels under the name of Fifi la Boom Boom, beginning with *"Oxana's Travails in Oxford,"* which won the International Prize for Steamy Bondage in 2001, followed soon after by *"Belinda's Travails in Brisbane," "Shania's Travails in Shanghai"* and his most recent work, *"Grizelda's Travails in Grimsby,"* which has already topped the Australian best-seller lists and has had similar results throughout Europe where it has been translated into fourteen languages.

Mr Brown's publisher has indicated that his client is working on a new book, believed to be entitled, *"Magdalena's Travails in Moscow."* A first printing is expected to be in the one million plus copies.

To date, he has refused to join the Australian Guild of Women Writers despite frequent invitations. However, prior to publication of this book, Leviticus Brown was reported to have told his brother that he was planning on joining the Guild under his pen name and then using his connections to be invited to appear on the television program, *"The World of Romance Novels"* on which he would, as he put it, "Reveal to the silly bitches that these best-selling novels were all written by a bloke and they're all exactly the same except for the names of the bloke and the shielah and the town where they get their kit off and have at it like rampant rabbits. It will make their bloody heads explode."

Stories from a Couple of Old Blokes

Death at the Opera House

History

Victor Takascz was born in 1922. He was in the second year of an apprenticeship at the Brno armaments factory when Nazi German troops overran the Bohemia and Moravia sectors of a small landlocked republic in 1938. When World War II was over, he applied for migration to Australia. He met Marla on the steamer, soon married her and settled at Lithgow, about 90 miles from Sydney in the Blue Mountains. He got a secure job at the Lithgow small arms factory. His son Petr, born in 1950 became a civil engineer.

Albert Green was born in 1921 at Chesterfield, Derbyshire. He was a foundry hand at the factory making small harvesters hay rakes and tedders. He was called up for service at eighteen years old in the Royal Electrical and Mechanical Engineers Regiment, and served in the North Africa campaign and conquest of Germany. He married Elsie. He applied for migration to Australia under the £10 scheme. He settled in Lithgow where he got a job in the workshop of a coal mine. He became good friends of the Takascz family after almost a year in a hostel for immigrants. His son, Chesterfield ("so you will never forget where you coom frum, lad!") and his daughter Emma married Peter Takascz.

* * *

The lad from Britain's industrial Midlands was proud of his family origin but preferred to be known as Chess in his new country. He acquired an interest in target rifle shooting particularly .223 or 5.56 mm, a calibre that R.T. (Ron) Marsden adopted for controlled experiments. Ron was in a select group known as "wildcatters" whereas Chess was a perfectionist in hand loading cartridges according to parameters evolved by precision gunsmiths.

Chess and Scots lass Janet lived together in a happy partnership that went back to final months at high school, their different interests contributing much to household harmony, she fond of things like macrame and making novelty ornaments from the shells glued together and carved with a Dremel tool. Janet even wielded a paintbrush now and again, her landscapes featuring in galleries.

Chess had a clerical job in a council office while Janet worked for an insurance company and they rented a one bedroom apartment at Marrickville, both hoping to break away from stultifying living offered by suburban Sydney for a much better life in the country where Chess wanted to have a small fodder crop farm. It all became possible when Janet scored her cut of a substantial windfall from a Lotto syndicate to boost what they had in the kitty. Both put their poorly remunerated jobs behind them and headed for the New South Wales central west where the region round Mudgee is synonymous with large-scale fruit and vegetable growing, grazing and wineries, popular with holidaymakers and tourists who have a wide choice of motel and hotel accommodation in a neat market town.

They secured a motel suite for three nights, picked up helpful literature from the Department of Agriculture local branch on small-scale farming and then presented themselves at a stock and stationery agency next morning after a country breakfast. Chess disclosed what he and Janet had in mind – a property much larger than the popular concept of a weekend hobby farm but nowhere the size needed for a viable grazing venture. They considered something in the order of between forty and seventy acres would be ideal.

The agent had only one mini–property listed, a lot of fifty-five acres in battle axe form near the hamlet of Running Stream between Mudgee and Lithgow. The "handle" was a fenced track of fifty yards, opening out to reveal an almost idyllic scene complemented by an 1890s weatherboard homestead whose corrugated iron hipped roof and panels of wrought iron lace made it the most beautiful building Janet had ever seen.

They wanted this property – no need to see anything else. Janet homed in on the very latest coke–fired slow combustion stove in the huge kitchen which doubled as living room. Abundant heat for comfort in winter, all cooking and hot water. Janet had her grandmother's recipe books and looked forward to creating great tucker the old way. An orderly kitchen garden and a short line of fruit trees promised the delight of home-grown food.

Storage of rainwater was more than adequate in tanks set into the ground, only their tops visible. A Southern Cross windmill pulled up irrigation supplies when needed from a creek never known to run dry. Chess noted there was a Massey Harris lightweight tractor in the machinery shed quite suitable for calling harvesting raking, aerating and baling equipment available in good second-hand condition from a major outlet in town.

Seeding and fertilising two distinct paddocks for turn and turn-about mode leading to cropping, got the nod from the agent who could see that Chess had given a lot of thought to being a farmer. Both effort and reward were to be spread over most of a year, allowing ample time for other interests.

A builder carried out a thorough inspection of the dwelling, shed and the boundary fencing and was able to issue a good report while a pest exterminator confirmed there was no evidence of white ants or borers. Purchasing their Nirvana went ahead, leaving legal people to attend to matters of title and transfer of money from purchaser to the vendor. They returned to Marrickville and began to sever all connections with suburban Sydney, spurred by positive viewpoints from the Takascz and Green families.

A caravan was put on site and rented for a fortnight following their return to Running Stream, allowing time to assemble furnishings that suggested the Edwardian era, commensurate with the age of a beautiful old Homestead. Between second-hand dealers in both Mudgee and Lithgow, they scored everything they needed. Janet's pride was her kitchen table capable of seating twelve which must have come from a farm supporting a large family, while Chess reckoned his magnificent roll-top desk could have been the pride and joy of somebody of note.

They always wanted to keep a dog but it wasn't a proposition until life in the country became possible. The RSPCA pound had a never ending population of unwanted animals clamouring to be adopted, jumping up against the Cyclone wire mesh the moment potential buyers were in the offing. Only one didn't put on a noisy show, her name was Penny, a six months old desexed female, smooth coat with a milk chocolate hue and a lot of kelpie in her. Penny offered a quiet "woof" to greet buyers, looked them up and down and seemed to say, *get me out of here, give me one good feed and plenty of fresh water every day and you'll never regret selecting me.*

With Chess at the wheel of the Nissan King Cab Utility truck, they returned home with the week's shopping in boxes on the rear seat and Penny curled up on the floor. As soon as they stopped and opened the doors, Penny hopped out, headed for the Homestead, did the circuit of the all-round veranda before she was off to the machinery shed and then back to Chess and Janet, another happy "woof" indicating her new home and environment pleased her.

Stories from a Couple of Old Blokes

As a competitor in Free Class, Chess had done pretty well over the years, but now wanted to devote more time to R&D. There was an ideal spot adjoining the kitchen garden for a rifle range just 150 yards long, actually six inch PVC tubing set into a trench. There would be a waterproof dugout at the firing end in which something remotely resembling a firearm was a test bed for evaluating all components and data shown up on targets illuminated by strong lighting wound out and retrieved on blind cord runners. Chess had built a mind picture of his range many years before and now everything fitted itself into the whole very smoothly. Brother-in-law Petr volunteered his professional advice and even helped with some of the spadework to tidy up what the trench digger left behind.

Their new lifestyles suited all three particularly well. No sense of urgency for anything. Neighbouring property owners make them welcome, firstly the women inviting Janet to a round of afternoon tea parties, then the blokes getting together after sundown once a week to ease the tops off a stubby or two. It all meant acceptance into a little community and making new friends for life.

It made sense to set aside the two smallest bedrooms that would be Janet's studio, as she wanted to call it, and an indoor workshop for Chess. Two bed frames and mattresses on the all-round veranda proved to be popular with visitors most of the year, a "sleepout" having just about disappeared from modern residential buildings.

The mini range functioned to expectations, noise factor more or less absorbed within the ground and not noticed by neighbours. In any case, a "silencer" attached to a rifle muzzle was ineffective when muzzle velocity exceeded the speed of sound, or around 1050 feet per second. In his program of evaluating data for his .177 project, Chess's chronograph would be registering a blistering 4250 feet per second. Wildcatters the world over were thankful for the malleable character of brass (an alloy of copper and zinc) which allowed it to undergo cold working for swageing the necks of cartridge cases to accept projectiles of a smaller diameter, using a bench top press and specialist dies.

When Chess came in for lunch after a forenoon in his machinery shed, Janet handed him a certified mail package delivered that morning by the Post Office contractor. It was a Friday. Briefly, the package came from Canberra, headquarters of the Australian Federal Police, requesting his presence in connection with Homeland Security generally but seeking helpful advice from a very successful exponent of Free Class marksmanship. There would be comfortable accommodation in police barracks and access to 24 hour cafeteria service. Open-ended travel vouchers were enclosed. *Your liaison will be Inspector Harry Doolan*, said the note. *You will like him – he did very well at shooting in the recent Fire Brigade, Ambulance and Police Games.*

Leaving his partner without transport was out of the question and not wanting to involve any neighbours meant Chess had to book a Mudgee taxi for the trip to the local airport for a flight to Sydney and connecting with the mainstream service to the Capital. He rang the AFP to let them know he would be on site before midday on the Monday.

Whereas Chess was a chubby man barely 5 1/2 feet in height, Doolan was a huge bloke, every bit of 6'7" and able to put the springs in bathroom scales under stress at seventeen stone. When a meeting got under way, it didn't take the visitor long to realise he was one of the new squad of ten, drawn from Australian Secret Intelligence Service (ASIS) and Australian Secret Intelligence Organisation (ASIO) field operatives, Australian Federal Police (AFP) and a couple of sundry others of definite Middle East appearance. An agenda forecast that two or three days would be needed to deal with a host of items while they had access to Chess.

It became blatantly obvious that the Q Team as it was to be known already knew everything of Chess's background, which at first surprised him before waking up to the fact he was in the company of cloak and dagger types whose job it was to know everything bordering on security. Chess was ordered to be secretive. He would be paid an annual retainer of $10,000 to carry out the bidding of Section Q but was more likely to be one of neutralising hostage-takers rather than assassinations as ordered by the Director with or without the concurrence of the Prime Minister when time was of the essence. This status would be that of Specialist Civilian Marksman (SCM) carrying a warrant card as issued to members of the AFP. His fellow team members were fascinated to hear from Chess that he could put a shot into the size of a ten cent coin out to 150 yards with his equipment featuring a tuned rifle, carefully hand loaded ammunition and his Nightforce 8 to 32 magnification NXS model telescope sight, a rugged instrument with the finest quality optics.

The shooter's early days in organised shooting sport interested the Q Team. An Australian rifle club formed under ARC regulations pursuant to the Defence Act of 1903 required its members to give under oath a lifetime commitment to assist in the defence of Australia. The young Commonwealth acquired leases of land for rifle ranges and there was some ammunition of old stock. All in all, it was cost-effective and reflected the vision of the founding fathers who were well aware of the vulnerable situation of a tiny population (under four million) in a huge land mass.

All was reasonably well until 28 April 1996 when Martin Bryant unleashed mayhem at Port Arthur, Tasmania, going berserk with firearms and killing thirty-five visitors to the historic site. Upgraded firearms laws resulted in the rifle club movement with which Bryant had no connection became the brunt of Federal government vehemence. The 1903 act was repealed and the Commonwealth cancelled its leases on land used for rifle ranges wiping out ninety-four years of loyal service to Australia, leaving only thousands of oaths that nobody could revoke and at a time when the planet was fast becoming a most unsafe spot.

Inspector Doolan – a born leader – and his versatile team derived a lot of benefit from the initial visit by Chess and so the director of intelligence agreed to make it an annual thing if more urgent matters hadn't surfaced. While the front line operatives were issued with army–type assault rifles fitted with low powered telescopic sights and performed most satisfactorily, more information on aiming techniques, for example, might enhance performance.

Hunters frequently had to shoot their quarry at an elevated or depressed angle. Armed with a stick of chalk and using the lecture room blackboard, Chess demonstrated why it was that the target eighty yards distance and at an angle of 25° would have to be regarded as being at seventy-three yards. It was tied in with a line of sight as against trajectory. His new friends appreciated the little tips that their visitor offered and they enjoyed witnessing the effects of likely charged cartridges that became "fizzers," no more harmful than kiddies' sparklers. At the other end of the scale, violent explosions under controlled safety procedures showed what happened if propellant made only for short barrel pistols and revolvers was inadvertently loaded into rifle cartridges.

* * *

The years rolled by. Chess and Janet were now sixty but there was no thought of retiring. Where could they go?

What would they do? Calling it a day was out of the question while both remained in good health. Janet even talked about offering morning and afternoon teas. Pots of black leaf tea, freshly baked rock cakes, local butter and local milk. She would launch her ideas next spring. Meanwhile, Chess had season after season of bounteous harvests.

Penny was beginning to show signs of old age, the hairs around her chin and chops looking grey and she was much slower than when she was trying to stab her jaws on pestiferous flies in summer heat. The loyal companion was heading for her eleventh birthday.

It was understandable that initial reaction to the 9/11 destruction of New York's Trade Centre Twin Towers was taken as promoting a Hollywood "blockbuster." It was all too bizarre to be anything else. Janet thought for a moment before saying 9/11 will be like a bookmark in a history book. The world wasn't a happy place at any stage. Belligerence, hatreds, greed and one-upmanship were dominant things which most nations were good at doing. Now, international terrorism had arrived to compound all the worst features in the psyche of human animals. It surprised Chess to hear his partner expressing her opinions so well. He thought his quiet little lady had no interest in international affairs because ordinary people generally felt it was pointless attempting to reverse trends.

Three weeks later, on a Sunday afternoon when Sydneysiders and visitors from all over were out and about to enjoy an iconic modern Opera House, the restaurant at its northern end overlooking the harbour was the site of a hostage incident. A terrorist had grabbed a young pregnant woman, positioned himself in front of a pillar and was holding a ferocious looking knife against her throat. Canberra didn't recognise the villain and were uncertain about connections, there being several wacky groups at both ends of the political spectrum apart from the more likely origin of the Middle East.

It was cooked breakfast time at tranquil Running Stream when the director phoned Chess, needing him to immobilise the terrorist for interrogation to be possible while avoiding any risk to the woman who was understandably distraught and in an advanced state of shock. A police helicopter was on its way to collect the SCM and his gear of .177 rifle, NXS scopesight, laser range finder and a block of ten rounds of ammunition marked with distances from 100 to 150 yards.

The chopper touched down on the green area adjacent to the northern pylon of the Bridge at Kirribilli where the Water Police were waiting with a launch. People in pleasure craft and the TV news crews and passengers in Sydney Ferries had an excellent view of what was happening onshore and didn't notice that the launch coxswain was manoeuvring his craft in the main shipping lane for Chess to have a clear shot between railing fixtures surrounding the Opera House perimeter.

Chess focused on the assailant's right elbow, checked the range finder disclosing a distance of 124 yards, picked up one round of ammo, loaded it into the breach and squeezed the light trigger. Through the powerful lenses of the NXS he saw the effect of disciplined marksmanship. Two things occurred almost simultaneously. First, the little .177 projectile ripped through skin, muscle, bones and tissue until sudden deceleration caused an implosion, radiating massive shock waves which left the arm hanging by ruptured tendons until the last one gave way, dropping an obscene blood covered limb to the ground, the hand like a giant claw still holding the knife.

Several female onlookers fainted and others including males threw up. AFP operatives pounced on the assailant and hustled him away to be processed. Central District Ambulance paramedics quickly wrapped the freed hostage in blankets and took her to hospital. Chess returned home in time for 1:30 Sunday lunch – an Australian baked dinner cooked to perfection in Janet's fuel stove, followed by afters of rice pudding. He wouldn't say anything about the assignment.

News telecasts that afternoon from four television channels advanced diverse opinions on the origins of a "miracle shot" that came from nowhere, the sound of firearm discharge being dispersed over a large body of water. One channel went so went so far as to suggest use of a "death ray" reputed to be under development and testing by the CSIRO. In the best interests of Homeland Security, the government did not offer any explanation, only saying that professional law enforcers were equipped to handle all acts of terrorism as they occurred.

They were variables and inconsistencies when handling precision ammunition that could be taken care of by "batching" but one inconsistent elements largely overlooked by all but a very few at the top of the game is the capacity of brass cartridge cases determined by thickness of brass for a chamber where fast burning propellant creates a sudden volume of gas to blow a projectile on its way. The only way to determine capacity is with a pipette and water, a time-consuming but thoroughly enjoyable exercise. It was another tip from their SCM that made Chess popular with the others in the Q Team.

Their living room was a setting for great commotion when Chess went back inside after a session in his dugout. A drivelling junkie was demanding money from Janet who politely told the intruder that cash wasn't kept at home because everything was paid for by the EFT and would he please buzz off, a request reinforced by Penny who had a firm grip on one of his ankles until copping a fatal heavy kick.

Eyeing a round of .223 ammunition, the unwelcome visitor wanted it for his Ruger sporting rifle. It looked pretty, its polished brass case marked with stripes made with a bright red wick pen left over from the periodic trips to Canberra which included a demonstration for Chess's colleagues in the Q Team.

About a fortnight after the domestic incursion, travellers on the road to Lithgow reported on offensive odour to a roadside maintenance gang, in all probability coming from a dead kangaroo that had been struck by a vehicle. The foreman said his gang would attend to the matter next day.

They found a human body in an advanced state of decomposition. The badly mutilated right-hand was with the remains of a rifle whose barrel and stout steel of its mechanisms had blown apart and driven the bolt backwards into the right side of the face, almost pulping it. A paper target nailed to a tree was flattering in a light breeze.

The junkie wasn't a competition shooter and so he had never heard the golden rule of accredited hand-loaders – never fire any ammunition made by somebody else. You don't know what is inside the brass case.

© Ian Young (aged 89)

My Life As I Remember It

Born October 18 1927.

The first thing that I can remember, it was 1929, I was about one and a half years old. We were coming from Detroit to live with grandfather Kiell. At the corner of the Concession #6 road and the Accommodation Road there was part of an old cheese factory crane for lifting 30 gallon milk cans off the wagon into the factory. The factory was gone just the crane was left. I can remember that.

The car Father had at the time was a five passenger hard top coupe V12 Cadillac I remember clearly being on the bench seat behind the driver's seat one time after we got here when the engine would not run. I remember where it was parked, out of the way as it could not move. That is the only thing I remember about that car or the trip here.

I remember holding this chicken a year or so later, too. I remember grandfather Lawson coming from Detroit about the same time as I held the chicken. I remember riding on my jumper (a four wheel kids riding toy) when they were getting out of the car. That jumper thing was around here for fifty years till I wanted to restore it.

I remember walking to school the first time by myself. Would have been in the first couple of weeks. There was a dark cloud in the sky and I thought it would rain so I went home. I was half way to the school when I turned and went home.

Grandfather Kiell being a blacksmith, I learned to temper steel. At twelve years old I made a chisel type drill tempered it and with a hammer drilled a hole through the six inch thick stone at the back door. The stone is still there. I step over the hole every time I go in or out.

When I was thirteen. I made a horseshoe from an iron bar, complete with a groove for the nail heads and square holes for nails, turned heel corks and blacksmith welded toe cork.

My shoe hung in the shop and when my grandfather passed they cleaned out the shop and tore it down. My shoe was gone.

When I was fourteen, I got my first job when school was out at the end of June 1942 as Water Boy at Murphy's quarry for McGinnis & O'Connor, a road building contractor. They built ten miles of Hwy 15 from Barriefield to where the prison gate is now at Joyceville. That ended in mid September and still fourteen, I got a job with the

Department of Highways Ontario doing surveys to see where HWY 401 was going to be built between Gananoque and Kingston. By the summer of 1943 the 401 job was finished and we were working on HWY # 7.

In the fall of 1943 my father opened the feed mill at Washburn, in an old wheat elevator in November. In March of 1944 I quit the survey job and came home to work in the mill. So at sixteen I'm running a grist mill and a Hydro Electric Power plant. I did that for twenty-five years. In 1945, the Township bought a road grader and my father got the job running it. I bought an electric welder about 1957 and learned to weld, I got welding torch couple years later. The mill is a museum now and a few times a year they ask me to give a talk on the history of the mill and area. The elevator was built in 1860. The Rideau Canal was finished in 1832. (No I was not there at the time)

Summer of 1947. I was shooting at lily pads in the bay when a friend lit a cigarette put it in his mouth and said shoot it out. So I did.

The only Christmas in eighty eight years I didn't make it home. Christmas Eve 1947 I was in Kingston fifteen miles from home on a motorcycle and a very bad snowstorm started it was so bad I had to go to a hotel for the night and had a very hard time getting home the next day.

In 1960 Mother and dad had friends from Michigan stop to see them. They were archers and showed me how to shoot a bow and arrow. We started an archery club and had the best field range in eastern Ontario. In 1971 I went to Vermont to an archery instructor school and in 1972 got a job at Queens University as the archery instructor coach. I was there for fourteen years till two of the four universities cut the funding for their archery program. I got to know a lot of great girls and still talk to a lot of them.

 Another learning something. Some time around 1977, the Queens girls gave me a Chinese cook book for Christmas. My son Allen must have seen the book as he gave me a wok. We had a glass top stove so I could not use the wok. Had to put in a counter top gas stove. The cooking turned out so good I now have three restaurant woks and a big gas stove for them and made a six bin hot table. Made a table to seat sixteen for the dinners I do.

In 1968 my father died and they (the township) asked me to take the job of running the grader, which I did for twenty-seven years till in May of 1995 I had to have a bypass. Learned a lot on that job, how to run backhoe, bulldozer and loaders' dump trucks. When I got back on the job after the operation, they said - their words - "When your sick leave is done, you're done," so ending twenty-seven years of leaving my mark.

One time a government inspector came checking on a road we had just finished building and asked the superintendent who had set the grades. The super said, "That guy in the grader." The Inspector said, "He sure did a job on them, 100%."

I remember my longest working day, February, 1993. I got the snow call and started 3:30 am, shut down 2:30 am the next morning. Twenty three hours, only stopping for fuel, three times, grabbed a bite and eat on the road.

My longest day: up at 6:30 am, left Guelph, Ontario at 7:00 am, 220 miles from home. Once home, I unloaded the van. Went fifteen miles and loaded ham radio stuff for a ham radio feast. Left around 5:00 pm and at 7:00 am we were in Fredericton, New Brunswick, 690 miles from home. By 7:30 am we were unloaded and set up for the show. Got to bed at 8:30 pm. 38 hours, a long day.

As I look back on my life there are a few things I feel bad about. One would be my poor spelling because of one teacher, eight grades in a one room school with an average of fifty three kids a year. He couldn't get to everyone.

The job that I consider my greatest achievement. My neighbour's wife wanted a log home, so in 1990 he and I built her one in one year.

At 89 I have found life has been a learning process, and I'm still learning.

Now for the pictures of the house-building.

© Copyright Kieth Keill (aged 89)

Stories from a Couple of Old Blokes

Above: The Beginning

Below: The Front Door -1

Above: Front Door – 2

Below: Begin Upstairs

Front Door – 3

Below: The End

Stories by the Kids

A collection of short stories written by young

people around the country

Henry the Hippo and Pluck the Chicken

One day, one of the hippos in the hippo club decided to go on a holiday. First, he came across a big red rock called Uluru.

"How fascinating," he said. Next, he found a farm and saw a chicken.

"Hi!" said the chicken. "I'm Pluck! Who are you? I can tell you're a hippo, but what's your name?"

"I don't have one," said the hippo.

The chicken looked startled.

"No name?" he said. "Well, I'll name you. How about Henry the Hippo?"

The hippo started to think. "Hmmm, I love it!" he yelled. "Want to come on holiday with me?" he asked.

"Yes!" said the chicken. "Let's go!"

On the third day, they came to a place called a zoo.

"Hmmm," they both said then Henry said, "Let's go!"

"Okay," said Pluck, scuttling after.

"Wow!" Henry said, "this place is terrible, all the animals are in cages."

"Not for long," said Pluck with a brave look on his face.

"Dun, dun, dun," said Henry.

"Pluck to the rescue!" screeched Pluck. "Pluck bock!" he yelled.

The people all ran away in horror, for Pluck was all fluffed up and angry, very angry. He stole the keys and set all the animals free.

On they went, passing great places like the Eiffel Tower, the Great Barrier Reef, the Great Wall of Gum and their favourite place, the Savannahs. But just for one particular place, they stopped and looked. Their faces looked like this: O_O.

"What's this mystical brown blob?" said Pluck.

"I think it's called poop," said Henry.

"Can we eat it?" asked Pluck.

"I think so," said Henry.

So they started to chew.

"Yum!" said Pluck.

"Yucky!" said Henry. "Oh well."

So they kept on moving.

They stopped again at a museum and saw many great things. They saw a dinosaur skeleton of a T-Rex and sixteen fossils but they didn't know the museum was closed. In came a burglar and stole all the sixteen fossils.

"Hey!!!" shouted Henry. "What are you doing?"

"Huh?" said the burglar. "A talking hippo?"

Pluck butted in. "Why, yes, and I'm the amazing Pluck the Magnificent, I sing and do autographs, too!"

And with that, the burglar jumped out of the window, screaming, "Mummy! Save me!"

"Mmmm." said Pluck. "Maybe next time you'll want an autograph. I'm okay with two o'clock."

"We'd better go to sleep," said Henry. "It's getting dark."

"Okay," replied Pluck, and off they went.

The next day, they woke up on a truck.

"Mmmm," said Pluck. "You didn't need to kidnap me for an autograph, huh."

His voice faded in the air.

"Okay," said Henry. "We're stuck, and I don't want to jump off this truck."

"Me, neither," said Pluck.

They stopped at Tokyo.

"I know where we are," said Pluck. "This is Japan."

"RICE!!!" screamed Henry and ran over to a table covered with rice and shoved it into his mouth.

Pluck came over.

"What are you wearing?" asked Henry.

"It seems to be a crown of good luck," said Pluck, who was wearing a bandana.

"Hmmm," said Henry. "Where will we sleep tonight?"

"A farm!" yelled Pluck. "A farm!"

"Okay, okay," said Henry. "We will."

© Audrey Eades (age 9)

The Big Little Book of Happy Sadness

George with a dog named Jeremy.

Once at the table, George thought that he would make a leg for Jeremy.

First he made a paper leg, but it got wet and ruined.

Next, Grandma made a pastry leg for Jeremy but he kept eating his pastry leg. He ate it all until it was all gone.

Next, George made a leg with a wheel to go play soccer.

Then George made a leg with a slipper on the end to go to bed.

© Navaeh Land (age 7)

Dungwarayayaka

In a deserted western part of an Australian landscape, were three aboriginal brothers hunting for food as a tradition lifestyle for these type of *Koori*. This has been a way of life for more than 5000 years.........

A rifle pokes out the window of a four-wheel-drive. Hunting with the old and the new styles of weapons, the rifle sight has been expertly attached with kangaroo skin.

CRACK! A shot rings out across the golden like dust and the chase is on. The 4WD accelerates, weaving wildly in and out of the dusty plain and over the roots of old bangalow trees.

"Having a nice ride everyone?" yells Hamzah Taylor, 17, his iPod plugged into the car's stereo system, and he turns up the volume in the car and switches the song to rock music through the 4WD.

His two brothers in the back are called Yikoom and Munyuk, they are both fifteen and they are both annoying at times.

"Hey can we help?" yells Munyuk.

"Yeah, can we help? We've gotten pretty good over autumn, mate," yells Yikoom.

"Yeah sure, why not?" replies Hamzah. Hamzar is the eldest and has decided to go hunting with his younger brothers.

BANG! koom and Munyuk have started to shoot at the camel behind the big wattle tree. BANG! BANG! Another shot at the wattle tree. Now the camel is really frightened and with that the camel starts to run, trying to dodge the bullets and fleeing to the other side of the plain. Hamzah stops the 4WD, gets his gun out and pulls the trigger and CRACK! The bullet goes flying and hits the camel in the neck and it slowly falls to its knees.

"You got it," yell the twins. The 4WD races over to the camel and they jump out of the car to take a look, and I'm not even going to say anything about this, it's just too gross!

* * *

One and a half hours later

The boys finally return back to their village with the big camel hanging of the side of the 4WD. They all jump out of the car with big grins on their faces. They walk towards the campfire to meet ever-smiling elder Menagarwoo Taylor, who is in her mid-60s. She remembers her childhood, which was at about the time of the Martu's first contact with whitefellas. She enjoyed hunting and gathering, and traveling with a family group of nearly twenty. Reliable waterholes and waterfalls were up to a day-and-a-half's walk apart, and Menagarwoo says they would often travel at night because when the moon hit the water it sparkled and made it clear for her to see through the water.

Nyalangka says that she would take them there at spirit time and go swimming with them.

"Dinner's ready," yells Nunga. Everyone sits around the campfire and starts to eat their meal. It's full moon tonight so everyone is going to celebrate by dancing round the campfire. Munyuk is dancing with the fourteen year old girl.

"Munyuk and Sierra sitting in the boab trees K.I.S.S.I.N.G!" sings Hamzah, happily. Munyuk's face turned a bright pink with embarrassment, so did Sierra's. But sitting in the corner is Yikoom, his face red with anger and overcome of jealousy of his twin brother. Yikoom loves Sierra too and had soon found out who she likes and it wasn't him.

The night starts to eventually sink down into the mountain and that was the sign that it was time for bed. Everyone goes to bed and hunting will begin again in the afternoon.

* * *

"Sierra," Munyuk whispers. "Sierra."

Sierra slowly starts to sit up straight. "Is everyone asleep?" she asks.

"Yes" he whispers back.

"Ok, let's go," she says. Sierra starts to climb down from the top bunk and they both slip out of the tent. They walk along a dirt path lit by the moon to make it look like sparkling water. After about five metres they stop and stand next to a big wattle tree, then look around to see if anyone is watching and start kissing each other. But close by is Yikoom, he has been hiding inside a big hollow log, his face red with anger and jealousy. He has been watching the whole thing and now he wants to destroy their relationship even if it means death.

109

* * *

The sun starts to climb up the sleepy mountain, giving the signal that it is time to pack and get ready to travel up the mountain to the sacred waterhole of the ancient rainbow serpent, so that the Koori can bath in it at midnight when the moon is full and shining on the water to make it magical. And this magic is used to heal the injured, make the old young again and to give wisdom. The tribe will be going up there to heal a sick toddler and to give the brothers, Yikoom and Munyuk and any other youths in the tribe, wisdom. But Yikoom, Munyuk's brother, is going to use this wisdom for bad and not for good because of his jealousy towards his brother and Sierra. For he too loves Sierra and he is willing to do anything to keep them apart even if he has to strangle his own brother for her.

Everyone is now ready to go up to the mountain and have started to go on their journey until they had realise that Munyuk and Sierra are missing.

"Hey, has anyone seen Sierra and Munyuk this morning?" yells Hamzar to the tribe. For a second no one answers until Yikoom raises his hand and says, "I saw them last night by the bangalow tree about five metres from the tent on the west side."

Sure enough, as Yikoom had told them, Sierra and Munyuk are sleeping under the bangalow tree. Everyone starts to laugh at them and with shock they both wake up, grasping each other at the sight of the amused crowd.

© Miriam der Kinderen (aged 13)

Regret

Prison was a boring place. The cold, grey, concrete walls had created no interest as the days, weeks, months and years ticked by. He knew there really wasn't anything like a life sentence.

He pressed his hands against the harsh, freezing iron bars that he was locked behind. If he could bend these bars, he would be free. Well, sort of. First, he'd have to stealthily escape and that's difficult when you're locked away in maximum security... If the guards opened fire, his old, weak body would soak up bullets like a sponge as the world slowly drowns around him.

No matter how much sludge they fed him, his mouth would still taste of regret. He started to wonder if his 'buddy' was still freely walking. If he could escape, the first thing he'd do was track down his old 'buddy' and have a little chat. After all, his 'buddy' was the reason he was here in the first place.

He peered through the small bars facing outward, onto to the courtyard. Pure darkness had swallowed the yard. He was starting to feel tired anyway. He climbed onto his rock-hard bed. He would do anything to sleep in a comfy, warm bed.

* * *

"Wake up sleepy, someone is here to see you, says he's a 'family friend'."

He suddenly woke to those words. He looked towards the guards standing at the prison door.

"What?" he stood up, as all the bones and his body cracked to remind him of his old age.

"You heard. A 'family friend' is here to see you." The prison guard looked at him, before turning around and walking out of sight. "All clear, bring him in!"

Suddenly, he realised exactly who was here to see him. He could sense him, he could feel the rage building up inside him.

Footsteps. He guessed there were probably three or four people heading his way. Two guards came into sight, before a shady figure wearing a long black trench coat and a black fedora came into view. He was exactly how he remembered his old pal.

"Here he is. You have five minutes, make it snappy," one guard nodded in the prisoner's direction.

He wondered how the guards had let him in. He looked very suspicious. The type you would think gets away with a life of crime. And that's exactly who this man was.

"Hello, old friend." His voice was gravelly, and emotionless, like old times. "Hello. Have you come to make 'a fair exchange'?"

Without making a sound, the newcomer reached into his coat, and pulled out a letter. It was flat, meaning it probably only contained a card, or paper. He slid it between the bars, waiting for him to grab it.

He yanked it out of his hands, and opened it with haste. A folded up piece of paper was inside. He pulled it out, and unravelled it. One word was printed neatly onto the page:

SORRY.

He looked back up, but the man no longer stood there. He was gone. Vanished. Something felt... different. He no longer felt angry, but sad. He knew it wasn't enough in exchange for a life in prison, but he knew whatever happened; his 'buddy' regretted it.

* * *

© Lachlan Coiner (age 12)

Garry

It was the dead of night but I was still awake. Suddenly I saw it. A big blazing, hot fire burning through the park towards my block of units. It had come from thin air. Suddenly there was silence and the fire disappeared again. I was curious but also scared. I tiptoed down the stairs and found a torch, a bag, some dry bread and cold meat and a flask full of water. I put on my high heeled boots, my long old ripped shorts, a t-shirt and a hat and jumper. As soon as I stepped outside, cold air rushed through me.

Then I heard a spine-tingling high pitched scream. I froze... I didn't dare move. After fifteen minutes I started moving again, this time more silently and I was more alert. I moved swiftly with the shadows. I gulped. There it was again. It was the scream. This time I kept on going. I didn't go on anywhere. I turned northwest and started moving. Why that way? I went that way because that was the direction the scream had come from.

I travelled for an hour and a half. When I came to a cluster of trees I put down my things and filled up my bottle from a nearby spring. Then I settled down and fell asleep straight away. When I woke up it was dawn. I checked my watch. It said 4:55am. I'd better start getting a move on, I thought. I got up and started moving. After several weeks I came to a dark, spooky, unfriendly wood. I went through it. Well not exactly all the way through, half way through. Then I found a cave. The cave was dark, gloomy and dusty. There was a loud snoring sound coming from in the depths of the cave. I entered. I wasn't scared, I was petrified by what I saw. It had sharp talons that could rip me with ease. It had huge paws that could knock over a building in a second. It had a paw actually, because on its left hand there was a hook that glinted in the sunlight. In his grasp there was a light green, beautiful, powerful sharp sword. In its handle there was a topaz. It was gorgeous, but deadly.

I name the monster Garry. He has huge yellow eyes, a short stubby blunt beak and big floppy ears. Garry is covered in light brown fur so he can blend in with his surroundings. He has short, stubby, fat arms and legs. Garry is very strong and has a lot of muscles that bulge up underneath his skin. I got out my arrows and longbow. I shot a dozen arrows at him, he was too quick and dodged all of the arrows.

Then he raised his massive talons ready to strike, but Garry had bad eyesight. He missed. Sparks flew as a great big fire started on the rocks behind me. Garry's sword cracked in half and fell into the ash and flames. I ran out of the cave into a tangled, smelly, quiet clearing. Garry followed me. He swung his hook at me. It caught my shirt. I got free though. Strangely, instead of jumping down to the ground I climbed up his arm onto his face and avoided his gnashing jaws. When I reached eye height I got out my knife ready to strike. Suddenly I lost my foothold and I fell to the ground. Luckily the ground was soft so I didn't hurt myself. I still had my dagger in my hand though. I hurled my dagger up towards Garry's eye. It hit him in the middle of the eye. He fell to the ground. Using the last of my strength I pushed Garry down the abyss, never to be seen again.

I went home. I was exhausted. I collapsed onto my bed and fell asleep immediately. I was tired. *Zzzzzzzzzzzzz.*

© William Hope-Jones, (age 7)

Rose's Castle

Once upon a time there was a little girl called Rose from lived by herself in a lighthouse. She was four years old and had been living by herself for a very long time.

She lived in a bedroom on the top floor right next to the big light that kept the ships away from the rocks below. She would switch it on and off when ships came past to keep them safe.

Rose was not lonely living on her own. Her parents had gone crazy and disappeared when she was three. So she had decided to find a new home where she could feel safe.

She had walked and walked until she reached the bush and saw a green bridge which she knew she had to cross. Then suddenly she saw her new home's light spinning slowly in the distance. It lit up a path for her, straight to its door.

No one answered when Rose knocked on the big wooden door. But when she walked in she found the table and a chair and a fridge full of all the things she liked to eat. There was chicken, noodles, spaghetti, ham sausages and cookies and a note saying, "Welcome to your new home!" She was so happy somebody had left all this food for her.

117

She ate a big dinner then went upstairs to the cosy little bed and fell fast asleep.

The next morning she went looking for a sailing boat she could take out onto the ocean. Rose wanted to get closer to the whales which were passing by. She found a little wooden boat, jumped straight in and headed out onto the bright blue sea.

When they saw her, the whales flicked up their tails and splashed all around as if they were seeing hello. They splashed her with so much water she fell out of the little boat! But that did not scare Rose. She had a big secret that no one else knew. As the waves swept over, Rose started to change. She started to grow the most beautiful glittering tail.

Rose was not scared of the ocean. She was not scared of swimming. What people did not know about Rose was that she was a mermaid as well as a little girl.

Soon it was Rose's fifth birthday. To celebrate, she was inviting all her mermaid friends. She swam from house to house under the sea and to each one she delivered a shell which popped open when they touched it. They were the most beautiful invitations Rose had ever seen.

Rose was very busy over the next few days. She organised a party band – a group of musical fish and a DJ.

Rose did not have parents on land, but underwater she had a mermaid mother and lived with her and five other mermaids in a castle made of sand, shells and coral.

On the night of the party, Rose put on a blue mermaid dress and in her hair she put on a new crown covered in green jewels.

Rose was really excited about her party, especially about the surprise she had for her friends. It was a box full of magic, including a magic wand.

When everybody arrived at the party they sat down to eat at tiny little tables. They had spaghetti noodles and chocolate cake. Everything was sparkly. Everyone was laughing and happy. But where was the music to dance to?

Rose got up, put her magic box on the stage and took out her magic wand. She waved it once and out came a microphone. She waved it three times and out came the band!

Now they had music to dance to!

Rose and her friends danced till they could dance more. Everyone said it was one of the best parties ever.

When all her friends had left, Rose suddenly realised she had a big decision to make. Could she go back to her life in the lighthouse after all the fun she'd had under the sea with her mermaid friends?

When she went to bed that night she could not stop thinking. But by the next morning she had made up her mind.

While Rose had loved her job as the lighthouse keeper, she realised she was lonely living on her own after all. She wanted all her mermaid friends and mermaid family around her.

She also wanted to live with her friends in a castle of her own. The next day she started building it out of sand, shells and coral with five of her mermaid friends. It was the biggest castle under the sea and the sparkliest one too. It was covered with hundreds of shells. Rose and her friends moved in after eight days and when she went to bed that first night and looked out of the window she could see the light from the lighthouse spinning high above the sea.

© Jade Butler

The Magic Tutu - an Extract

The sky was blue and not just any blue, the most amazing blue you've seen. From below the clouds looked like candy floss and the dog begged the Queen for some candy floss.

"Oh fine then," said the Queen and she hopped into the hot air balloon and she rose up and up and up until she could rip the cloud and they happily went home together and when they got home they both were very tired.

© Abigail Hope-Jones, (age 5)

The Bravest Little Viking

One night it was pitch black and nobody could see anything. I woke up lying on the ground. Mummy and Daddy had to go to work and after work, they had to go to an important meeting and I had to go to Granny's and Poppy's.

Mummy told Poppy not to tell me any scary stories. When I got inside, Poppy said, "Close your eyes," and then he gave me a book about Vikings. I read the first two chapters.

My dog and I wanted to be fierce Vikings just like in the book, so we will. My name would be Fiber the Fierce and my dog's name would be Nut the Fierce.

We went to the park to be fierce Vikings. Some of my friends were there, too.

They said, "What are you?"

I said, "We are fierce Vikings."

"We want to be fierce Vikings like you," they said.

"But you have to train really hard if you want to be real Vikings like us," I said.

Mummy and Daddy came to pick me up. Mummy said, "Did you have fun?"

"Yes," I said, "I had lots of fun, can I come again tomorrow?"

Mummy said, "Yes."

"Yaaaaaaaay!"

Everyone laughed.

The next day when I went to Granny's and Poppy's, when I got inside, Poppy told me to close my eyes and hold my hands out and then he gave me a real set of Viking armour. I wore it all day until Mummy and Daddy got there,

I said, "Mummy, Daddy, look what Poppy got me, a real set of Viking armour!"

Mummy and Daddy said, "Thank you."

Poppy and Granny said, "Bye."

The next day, I got in and Poppy told me to close my eyes and hold my hands out and then he gave me more Viking armour and I said, "Who is this for?"

"Your friends," said Poppy. "Go and give it to your friends."

I went back to the park hoping that they were there and they were and they dressed up and we were all Vikings.

© Naveah Land (age 7)

The Coat

In a desert land across many plains somewhere near the Mexican border, a handsome young boy, separated from his parents shortly after his birth, wore an extravagant coat painted with the colours similar to the Northern Lights and the beauty of rainbows. His name was William Russell but his friends knew him as Billy.

He was a poor fellow with nothing to his name but his mother's coat. Many people bid on his prized possession, but every time he declined their offers.

While trekking tirelessly, moving to a new town every week, his rations turned to nothing, but he would starve before he made the journey. One sip of water would give him the strength and determination needed to complete his hard day's scavenging. He looked for any sign of water but he heard only the winds howling and the sand stirring. He believed all hope was lost.

He contemplated all his life, believing he might die where he stood. A small breeze swayed his coat in an easterly direction. Hoping his parents wherever they might be were looking down on him, with tearing eyes, helping him. Without even noticing, he headed East until the coat became stationary once more.

With the little education he had received, he had heard of pockets of water forming below the sand and taunting him until finally, he desperately dug with his bare hands where he stood, clawing down deeper and deeper.

A little droplet that he found quenched his thirst and delighted him. Afterwards, he came to grips with the knowledge that he had lost his sense of direction and at least he could pass away in happiness and be reunited with his family. He closed his eyes and sighed, plunging into darkness.

Surprisingly, he awoke, hearing helicopters roaring and he was confused, but it didn't matter, nothing did. He was alive and throughout all of this he had kept his coat. It was then that William Russell realised he had a peace with his parents the whole time. That coat was passed through the Russell generations and everyone knew the household name, great grandfather William "Billy" Russell.

© Makyah Cusbert (Aged 12)

The Dolphin That Learned to Fly

Chapter 1

Once there was a dolphin family of five that lived in the Great Barrier Reef. Molie and Mark were the names of the parents. The names of the children were Jarod, Michael and Cari.

One day when Jarod was left in charge, Cari's sense of adventure kicked in.

"I'm going out to buy some bread, Jarod," Cari said.

"But mum and dad are out to buy the bread. Cari, are you lying to me?" Jarod asked.

"Ummm...." Cari started. "Of course not, Jarod, I...I...I just wanted to make sure they remembered the ummm... fish. Yeah, that they remember the fish!"

"All right, Cari," Jarod said. "But I'm asking mum and dad if you did or not."

"Okay," Cari said. "See you soon."

Once Cari knew that she was out of sight she looked for signs of adventure. After about two or three minutes she heard a whisper.

"Come to me, Cari."

Cari didn't hesitate and went straight to the source of the whisper.

"Who...who...who's there?" Cari asked, a little frightened.

"Me! Honey Bunny! Your long lost Aunt Fiona!" said a head that popped up from nowhere.

"Aunt Fiona, I thought you were dead!" said Cari.

"You know Cari, there's a big reef out there! I've found lots of fish in my years of disappearance but one found me! You!" exclaimed Aunt Fiona. "Hey, do you want me to show you something amazing?"

"Yeah, sure, what is it?"

"Oh, you will see... MWHAHAHAHAAAAA!"

"Okay."

"Come with me, Cari."

So Cari followed her Aunt to what looked to be an old wrecked pirate ship about twenty metres away, but what Cari didn't know was that she was about to see something extraordinary! She just had to wait. Once they got there Cari realised that they were not alone in this place, well there were only about two or three other animals there including, a shark, a fish, and something that looked like it was meant to be another dolphin. Anyway, Aunt Fiona showed Cari the most amazing thing anyone could ever dream of! It was how to fly!

"Wowser!" exclaimed Cari. "Can I have a go? Can I? Can I? Please?"

"Sure, sweetie pie!" said Aunt Fiona.

It took Cari quite a few days to master flying, but once she could do it easily, she realised that she actually didn't like it!

Chapter 2:

After she had stayed with her Aunt for a few days, Cari started to miss home, so she was about to set off when her Aunt told her that she would have to fly to get home for they had travelled so far away that they had lost track of home. Cari was so sad about not being home, she decided that she and Fiona would set off to fly back home, and Fiona agreed, so off they went on their long journey. They kept on going and going and going and finally Fiona realised that they were going the wrong way, so they turned back and started swimming.

Once they got back, Cari, Jarod, Michael, Molie, Mark and Fiona held a party. It was all fun until Molie remembered that her dad was also missing and they all turned to Cari and said in unison, "Go get him, dolphin!"

© Sophie Whittaker (aged 10)

THE GIRL IN THE SEWER

Lunah Kabble went missing the same day that three boys and two other girls did. They had been missing for days then the kidnapper struck again. Lunah was fiercer than the five other kids. They had grown weak and starving. They had told Lunah they were too scared to eat, sleep or drink. They had only just survived after living in the sewers for five days. Lunah had always been fierce and strong. But she had become fiercer and stronger after being kidnapped.

Lunah did not know her parents because they had died when she was four. She was adopted by mean people who didn't care about her the tiniest bit. As Lunah got older she started wondering why these people had adopted her. By the age of nine Lunah had become very brave and adventurous. She started to sneak into the forest behind her house and look around. Lunah was now ten. One night she had become lost deep in the forest. She saw a light and like a moth became attracted to it. She thought it may be her house. Once she came close to the light she it was a camp of tents. That's the night it happened. The night Lunah went missing. Lunah heard a child crying softly in a nearby tent. As Lunah was Lunah being curious and all, she wondered over to the tent. Then she felt cold hands grab her shoulders. She was shoved into the tent. She heard a click like a padlock locking. She turned around saw two girls and three boys all crammed into this tiny tent. In the corner she saw the girl crying. She looked up. She stifled a smile.

"Hi" she sniffed. "My name is," she sniffed again, "Sophia Minkle, what's your name?"

"I'm Lunah. Lunah Kabble."

The other girl about the same age as Lunah turned around. She had wavy ginger hair. She smirked.

"Am I like seriously the only one here with a normal last name? Because these jerks," she pointed at the boys, "have like dumb last names too!"

"Well what's your name then?"

"Ashley Hollis."

I walked over to a spare sleeping bag and plonked myself down. I landed on something hard. "Ouch," I muttered. I rummaged through the sleeping bag. I pulled out a small bag. A shadow fell over me. I glanced up and saw Ashley glaring at me. She snatched the bag from me and stormed over to her 'area'.

Right then I wished I were at home. Even though my adopted parents hated me, they still fed me nice food and gave me a warm bed. They provided me with toys and education. But they treated me horribly. They never took me places or let my friends come over for plays, or even let me go to friend's houses. The only place they let me go is school. They didn't even let me go into the garden. Either they had to know about the kidnappers in the forest or they did't trust me.

Luckily when I was kidnapped I had a bag with me. My school bag. I always bring it with me when I go into the forest. It contained my diary, a pencil case, a horse book, a packet of chips and an apple.

I woke up at about 6:30am. My usual time. All the others (except Ashley) had woken up. Sophia told me that Ashley likes her beauty sleep.

"Beauty sleep at age ten?" I ask.

"I know, dumb right?" Sophia giggled.

"Those three don't talk much, if at all, do they?" I said tilting my head towards the boys.

"They have never said a word the whole time they've been here!"

I giggled. It must have been louder than I thought because Ashley woke up. She sat up and pulled her sleep mask off.

"WHO JUST WOKE ME UP?!? HAVEN'T I TOLD YOU ALL ENOUGH TIMES THAT I NEED MY BEAUTY SLEEP!!!!!!!!!!!!!!!!!!!!!!!!!!!" Ashley yelled.

I heard the click of a lock and the tent zip was pulled up. I turned around and saw a person in black. He shoved a tray with six bowls of sloppy porridge into the tent.

"Breakfast," he grunted.

He zipped the tent up. I waited to here the click of the padlock, but I didn't. I realised that the person hadn't locked up the tent. Sophia and the boys had noticed too. I grabbed my bag and so did the others. Ashley was by now asleep again. I thought maybe we should leave Ashley behind. Sophia must have been thinking the same thing because she dragged me out of the tent.

"Wait," I whispered.

"Come on!" Sophia urged.

I tiptoed over to Ashley and packed up her stuff into a big pink backpack. I gently shook her. She stirred and sat up. Pulled off her eye mask and glared at me. "Come on, Ashley. They have left the tent unlocked. We are going."

"Whatever," Ashley said sleepily.

I dragged her out of her sleeping bag. She stood up and grabbed her bag. She flung it over her shoulder and we all ran out of the tent.

Last night, these kidnappers must have moved us somehow because we were no longer in the forest outside my house. We were now outside the sewers. I saw the boys running into a huge pipe, water splashing up behind them. Ashley and Sophia saw them too and we all started running towards the pipe. As we entered the pipe I heard splashing behind us. At first I thought it must just be Sophia, but I realised she was next to me. I looked behind me and almost crashed into a wall. A person in black was chasing us. I started screaming and so did Sophia. The people must have given up because the splashing got quieter. We saw light and so did the boys. We turned off and came to a big area.

I felt like I must have been running for an hour. I stopped and turned around to see how far behind the others were. The others were gone. Panic rushed around my body. I started to cry. I saw a dry part of concrete and I sat down, pulled out my diary and a purple pen. I wrote and wrote and wrote.

> *Dear Diary,*
>
> *I have been missing for three days now. I am stuck in the sewers and it stinks! There are these other boys who never talk and two other girls. A mean drama queen one called Ashley Hollis and a nice bubbly one called Sophia Minkle. But they have*

gone a different way than me. So now, I am lost! For some weird reason I feel like I am in the sewers near my house, but I doubt it. I don't really have much more to say except for the fact that I have not eaten for ages. I have an apple in my bag and some chips but that is all. I will have to ration. I am going to eat half of my apple now. Now I really don't have anything more to say to you. But if anything happens I will write it in you. So that I can forever remember this.

Bye!

LKabble

I closed my diary with a snap and stuffed it in my bag. I zipped it shut and flung it over my shoulder. I jog down the pipe, the same way I came before. By now my shoes and socks were drenched with stinky sewer water. I found the same tunnel that I went into before. But then I realised that I had taken a wrong turn. Out of a tunnel I passed I heard someone whisper. I stopped. I peered down the tunnel and saw a flash of ginger hair. ASHLEY! I ran as fast as I can.

"Quick!"

I recognised Sophia's voice. I followed the ripples in the water. I saw Sophia dash around a corner about fifty metres away. "SOPHIA, WAIT!" I screamed. I stopped and so must have Sophia, Ashley and the boys. I peeped around the corner. I saw them all just around the corner. Sophia ran up to me.

"We were looking for you everywhere!"

"Even Ashley?"

"Well no, not exactly..."

"What do you mean 'not exactly'?"

"She was... Okay no she wasn't helping," she said.

"It's just Ashley has started...um... being nice" she stuttered. I was shocked. So shocked I forgot how to speak.

We all walked for a while until the tunnel became narrower and narrower. The tunnel was dry here, so they to got comfortable and got some sleep. The concrete ground was really hard. Lunah sat up against a wall with her diary and a blue pen. She started to write.

> *Dear Diary,*
>
> *I have found the others now and we are having to sleep on very hard ground. Sophia brought a blanket. She is very comfy and asleep. Ashley is complaining and the boys are lying there as silent as usual. It is hard to write in the dark but luckily I found a torch in my bag. I am very tired so I'm going to sleep now.*
>
> *Toodles!*
>
> *Xox*

I put my diary away and laid down with my head on my bag. After about half an hour I fell asleep.

I woke up to the sun pouring down the narrow tunnel. The others were up and ready, even Ashley.

"We're going to go up this tunnel," Sophia said as she pointed to the narrow one.

"Okay," I said sleepily. I dragged myself though the tunnel. The others were full of energy. After about five minutes, I was up at the front, not tired the tiniest bit anymore. The tunnel ended outside a food shop. Ashley suddenly spoke into the silence.

"Let's rob it for food!"

"No!" Sophia shrieked. "Let's go to the police!"

"Let's have a vote." A boy's voice surprised us all. One of the boys had finally spoken!

"I agree!" Lunah said. So they all voted. Ashley and one of the boys voted to rob the shop for supplies. Sophia, Lunah and the two other boys voted to go to the police. So they went to the police.

It turned out that they were fifteen kilometres from their town, Zoolabah. And the other kids actually went to the same school as Lunah. Lunah was surprised she hadn't heard their names before.

When Lunah got home she wrote and wrote and wrote and wrote in her diary with a green pen.

Dear Diary

I'm back at home now and my room is nice and warm. My adopted parents have got a cute white kitten. Her name is Blossom. Even though I was only gone for six days my parents have got a kitten and a SPA! But they said I can't use it. I thought they'd be nice to me now. But obviously I was wrong! At least they give me nice food, pretty clothes, a warm room and a pet. But they don't give me cuddles or kisses. Nothing to show that they love me and nothing to show that I love them. Except one thing I did when I was five. I wrote a letter to them.

It read:

Too Mummy and Daddy, I miss yu wen im at pree sckool! Luv From Lunah xxxx

Now when think about I really wish I'd never of done that. Because when I was five I used to think my mum and dad loved me. So I wanted them to think I loved them back.

Then three years later, when I was eight, I found it in my parent's junk draw. Ever since I was eight, so for nearly three years, I've known that they hate me. Anyway I'm seriously tired right now. So I'm going to sleep in my warm bed.

Bye!

Lunah Kabble

Lunah fell asleep at 10:47pm. She slept until 9:11am. Her adopted parents let her have a day off school. Lunah walked off to the lounge and grabbed the newspaper. She glanced at the front article and nearly screamed in shock. Someone else had been kidnapped. The article read:

GIRL GONE MISSING!!

Lucy Lockhart went missing the same day that Ashley Hollis, Lunah Kabble, Sophia Minkle, Bryce East, Greg Hoffle and Rodrick Hoffle were found.

Lucy is six years old. Together the government and Lucy's parents are offering a $1000 reward for finding Lucy.

Please phone 0455 365 189 or 6580 900 657. Help find Lucy Lockhart!

Lunah knew what it was like to have been missing so she rang up the first phone number listed.

"Hello, Mrs Lockhart speaking."

"Hello this Lunah. Lunah Kabble."

"LUNAH!!! Oh hi! Have you rung up about my daughter, Lucy?"

"Yes I have. I just thought maybe you might want me to help you find Lucy. Because I think I know where she might be. But I will need your address."

"Okay. I live at 30 Water Terrace".

"Thanks."

Lunah hung up. Then I ran up to my room and packed my bag, sneaked to the garage and jumped on my bike. I rode to her house. It took about ten minutes.

Water Terrace is a posh road with a lot of modern or big houses. Number 30 Water Terrace is a big brick house. I dropped my bike onto the neatly mown grass, took off my helmet and ran up to the front door. I pressed the doorbell. DING!!!!!!!!!!!! I heared footsteps and a lady in a flowery dress opens the door.

"Lunah! Come in! Come in!" Mrs Lockhart said.

I wiped my dirty Converse shoes on the welcome mat. I stepped inside. It was so posh. And so huge. Mrs Lockhart led me into a big living room. I sat down on a comfy white lounge; it feels like I'm sinking into it. A fluffy white kitten, one that is identical to Blossom, jumped onto my lap.

"Oh yes, Lunah! Your parents got Blossom from here!"

"Really?" Lunah asked. Mrs Lockhart nodded. Her husband walked in carrying a tray of biscuits. They were the expensive, good quality ones. Lunah didn't like them. She only liked the cheap crumbly ones. "Anyway I'd better go investigate," she said quickly.

"Oh yes! Of course!" Mrs Lockhart said. I walked out the door and to my bike. I clicked my helmet straps together and jumped on my bike. I rode around the back of the house. I KNEW IT!!!!!!!!!!!!!! This all added up! Lunah pulled out a notebook and started writing down everything.

- The Lockhart's have a forest out the of their house.
- They also have sewers about 3kms away.

Lunah put her notebook and pen away. She leant her bike up against their back fence. As Lunah walked into the edge of the trees, she heard a familiar car engine. She peeped out of the trees and saw her mother and father running over to her bike.

"This is definitely her bike, Starry," Mr Kabble said. Mrs Kabble looked around at the trees and nearly saw Lunah's hand.

"Bob, look!" Starry pointed at Lunah's hand.

Lunah heard the grass crunch as Mr and Mrs Kabble crept up on her. She had no choice but to run, her backpack bobbing around. As she ran she saw loads of tents. She knew this was the right place. Lunah ran behind one of the tents and pulled out her note book. She wrote more information about what she had found.

⤞ The kidnappers are staying in the forest outside people's houses
⤞ They are also trying to stay near the sewers
⤞ They going start kidnapping little kids
⤞ I really need to find out who these people are

Lunah put her notebook and pen away. She stood up and snuck over to a gap in between some tents. As she looked around she noticed one of the tents had a padlock on the zip. Lunah pulled a bobby pin of her pocket. She quietly ran up to the tent. Luckily Lunah knew how to pick locks. The lock clicked open. She zipped open the tent and inside was Lucy Lockhart.

"HEY!!!!"

I turned around and saw a man running at me.

"Lucy! QUICK!" I hissed.

Lucy scurried towards me and we ran into the trees. We didn't stop running until I was sure the people were gone. When we got to the houses again I realised we'd come out fifteen houses away. Lucy and Lunah jogged all the way to the Lockhart's door. DING!!! went the doorbell. Mr Lockhart answered the door with Mrs Lockhart right behind him.

"LUCY!!!!!!!!!!!!!"she screamed. Mr and Mrs Lockhart and Lucy were all hugging each other.

"Lunah, thank you so much!" Mr Lockhart said in between tears of joy. He handed over $1000.

"This is for you, Lunah," Mrs Lockhart said. Lunah forgot all about the reward of $1000.

"No, no! Please you keep it!" Lunah gave the money back.

"Just take $100 then," Mr Lockhart spoke again.

"Just $100 then." Lunah took the money and began to walk home, which, without her bike took twenty minutes.

When Lunah got home she doodled in a notepad for half an hour. Once she got bored with drawing she decided to go to sleep even though it was only 6:32pm.

In the morning, Lunah ran out to the living room to get the newspaper. When she was back in her bedroom she read the front article:

LUCY LOCKHART FOUND!

Lucy Lockhart was found two days ago by Lunah Kabble. Lunah said to the Lockhart's that she might have known where Lucy was. Lunah refused to take the $1000 reward and instead took $100. Lunah will be getting an interview and will be on the news in one week.

KIDNAPPERS IDENTIFIED

The kidnappers have been found. Mr and Mrs Kabble wondered into the forest looking for Lunah.

They came across the kidnappers and called the police. They were caught 15 minutes before Lucy was found.

The kidnappers were two twenty year old men.

Anderson Brooks and Nathan Ling. They have gone to court and will now be in prison for 20 years.

No one had told Lunah she was going to be on the news in one week. And her adopted parents had caught the kidnappers? Lunah went to write in her diary with a pink pen.

Dear Diary,

I found the girl that was kidnapped. I got $100. What is weird is that my parents caught the kidnappers 15 minutes before Lucy was found. Unless that person chasing me was my father pretending to be a kidnapper. I doubt it.

Toodles

Xoxoxox

Lunah put her diary on her desk and got out a spare notebook. It was new. She had bought it with the money from her reward. She started to write a story.

Lunah Kabble went missing the same day that three boys and two other girls did.

© Jodie Barber (Aged 12)

Gravitational Orbitaria

The Galactarian forces' gargantuan mass outweighs the miniscule resentment our council portrays in comparison, and intergalactic conflict has subdued the galaxy through hardships of depression and loss as our Airatibro sector was diminished through warfare. Some wish to flee Gravitational Orbitaria, however we shall reside within this galaxy until all of its inhabitants cease to exist.

As squadron 05GRAV9 leaves, the Gravit Base resigns itself to a fate unimaginable as the violated base info gives the Galactarian forces knowledge of unfathomable value, which brings on the defeat of the entirety of the subterranean engulfed portion of the galaxy cornering a universe known to be very territorial and consists of five planets identified as Molten-Ra, Seaban-Tess, Gren-Ma, Ike-Bet and Gen-C not including the renowned Resistant Solitarion Gravity Craft (R.S.G.C) hidden in the far reaches of the universe.

"We endure troubles as the protection against combat isn't a liberty we have," said the President. "Precautions are highly advised but will provide little help because of the lack of trade routes after the demise of Planet Edart-Ecruos."

"This predicament has dumbfounded us, so my proposal is that we fortify our remaining frontiers in an attempt to prevail and corrupt their perilous ruling. As expected this plan was opposed, however conspiring later reasoned with the proposal and came to the conclusion of perusing this idea through secretive means.

"Fortifying a planet is complicated, however the inhabitants living in the resisting planets are highly resourceful. Fortunately the supposed planet to be targeted first is inhabited by a highly advanced intellectual and logically thinking race named after a god of the sea, Aquar-Mann. These Aquarians see logic within necessary fortifications as an attack is highly imminent. Due to Galactarian customs they reason in Barbaric terms, ultimately giving command to declare WarMonger (Eternity Of War.)

"Many goals are overly underestimated as difficult. We as the re-tellers of the story relay hope to the mighty god Gondalf's idealism and hope for Gravitational Orbitaria's peace and tranquillity."

© Makyah Cusbert (aged 12)

Once Upon A Mystery

Samantha Miller grabbed the newspaper and looked at the front page. It read:

Dog Missing!

```
Name:  Twinkletoes  -  last  seen  on  11
December  at  11 am  in  the  owners  back  garden
in  Washington  Street.  Reward  of  $300  for
any  information  leading  to  the  safe  return
of  the  dog.  Phone:  0496 111 043.
```

Sammi knew this was her last chance to get $300. So she went out into the neighbourhood to see if she could find the dog.

After walking around town for 10 minutes, she pasted an alleyway and noticed two men talking suspiciously. Sammi stopped to have a look and see if she could hear what they were talking about.

She carefully edged closer to the man. She couldn't quite hear them so she went back behind the then. When she heard the men talking she hit "Record" on her phone.

"I've got the dog in the back of the van," said the taller man.

"Where's the van?" said the short, moustached man. The tall man beckoned him to follow. As the men were leaving, one dropped his phone and didn't notice. Sammi run over to the phone and snatched it up. She stopped her phone recording and ran to the police station.

Inside the police station, Sammi spoke to the Duty Officer who called his sergeant to come and see the information which Sammi had. The sergeant was very impressed and thanked her for her excellent detective work.

Sammi left the station with the intention of going home until she saw the man again! They were on a private property next to a muddy white van. The moustached man saw Sammi and she wondered if he had perhaps caught sight of her in the alley.

Then the man got in the van and zoomed off. The town that Sammi lived in had not even ONE hill so she could see the van driving on for about five minutes.

"Hi Sammi!" she heard someone yell. It was her best friend like ever, ever, ever Jodie Barber. "What are you up to?" continued Jodie.

"There's a dog missing and I think I know who took it! There's a $300 reward for its safe return."

"That is epic as!" Jodie yelled as she ran across the road. She didn't even check before crossing, just narrowly missing a car. (Jodie was really into mystery and tomboy stuff. But she also liked make-up, looking pretty and that sort of stuff. Sammi and Jodie were really popular and they both had a boyfriend.)

Sammi and Jodie ran after the van.

They were led to a car park where Sammi and Jodie had once lost their bikes. But that was only two weeks ago. They saw the man lifting a cage out of the van.

"Is that the dog?" Jodie asked. Sammi shrugged in reply. Once the men had gone off through the trees, the girls ran over to the van.

"I'm going to take a picture of the numberplate," Sammi said. She took a photo and so did Jodie just in case something happened to Sammi's photo or phone. But as Jodie was taking the photo, the men came back and saw them.

"What do you think you're doing?" the tall man raged.

"Yeah!" said the moustached man.

"Oh great!" whispered Sammi.

"Quick, go to the bikes." Jodie whispered back. They ran to their long lost bikes and jumped upon the squeaky seats. They rode off along the straight and dusty road. In the distance they could hear the men chasing them down the gravelly path. The girls started to slow down as a field came into view. Near the closest side fence to them, there were three horses. One was chestnut, one was black and one was such a beautiful silver and white. The tail was white but as it got to the end, it became very, very, very, very light brown. Jodie was off her bike as soon as she saw the horses. Oh yeah, did anyone mention that Jodie loves horses?

"Red, hurry up! There is no time to stop, Red!" Red is the codename for Jodie and Gold for Sammi. They had decided not to use their real names.

It was nearly too late. The men lunged for the girls. Just in time they managed to ride off. Jodie was heartbroken at having to part with the beautiful white mare. They cycled off through some trees. There was dust flying in the air. It was obviously because the van containing Twinkletoes had just driven off. They cycled super duper speedily after the van that they could see in the distance. After about ten minutes they came to the edge of town.

The van stopped at an old farm with a big metal shed. The farmhouse was old and rotting away. It looked as if a big fire had swept through and destroyed everything. The shed appeared as though it had been repaired with big bits of metal. Jodie and Sammi chucked their bikes into an overgrown hedge. Then as quietly as quiet could be, they crept to the back of the metal shed; which was a mistake.

Around the back of the shed, they heard men's voices.

"I got the little golden Labrador," one said.

Jodie looked round the corner and saw the men.

"Good, we needed that one. It's rare," said a short but plump one.

One of the men opened the door and straight away the barking began. Jodie and Sammi tiptoed into the shed, Sammi hid behind some crates of dog food and Jodie climbed to the top of the shed, then sat in the loft. The men shoved a pretty little golden Labrador into a cage marked: TWINKLETOES.

Sammi counted how many dogs they were and wrote it down.

12 dogs:
German Shepherd: Max.
English Staffy: Rose.
King Charles spaniel: Charlie
Yorkshire Terrier: Trixie.
Two Poodles: Leonard and Fifi.
Golden Labrador: Twinkletoes.

Red Setter: Sunset.
Two Dalmatians: Jibber and Jabba.
Two Huskies: Sapphire and Gem.

Jodie took a photo of the dogs on her Fruitphone. Then the most unexpected thing happened. A man with a top hat marched through the big door. It was the mayor!!! The mayor is a short man with a small moustache. He always wears a suit with a large yellow tie. Why was he there? Could he found out about the dogs? Was he there to stop these people?

"Good, I see you've got that rare golden dog," the mayor boomed.

"Yes, but we have one problem," squeaked a rather nervous man. The mayor frowned then said in his booming voice, "What? What problem?"

"Well," started the nervous man. "Mr Bode rang me and said that two girls rode here. He... he... explained that... thatt they followed the van," he squeaked. The mayor's face went a deep shade of scarlet.

Jodie had got this whole conversation on video. Suddenly, all the dust in the loft made Jodie sneeze. This wasn't an ordinary sneeze, it was one of those where you didn't want to sneeze but you had to. Her sneeze was loud and it echoed round the small space of the metal shed.

Jodie knew they'd be found now. Sammi decided to risk it and run to the bikes. So, Jodie carefully climbed down onto the cages, then jumped off and ran after her.

She could see Sammi just ahead in the trees; the path was narrow and long. Sammi dragged the bikes out of a hedge and waited for Jodie. They rode off back to the old car park and had a rest for five minutes. They then continued to the main street. There were going to cross the road to the public bubbler when they saw Sammi's Auntie Krystal. She drove a big four-wheel-drive vehicle. Auntie Krystal stopped.

"What are you girls doing?" she asked.

"Auntie Krystal, we'll tell you in the car, just drive us to the police station," Sammi said. Auntie Krystal was very confused but listened anyway. Once the bikes were in the car, they drove off to the police station. Auntie Krystal said she would take the bikes to their houses.

Inside the station it was nice and cool. It smelt of strawberries and aftershave. They explained to the police officer why they were there. Sammi explained about the notes she had taken. It turned out that the dogs in the shed were all dogs that were missing and had never been found. Jodie showed her video of the conversation. The police officer was impressed that two eleven-year-old girls solved this mystery.

Meanwhile back at the shed, the men were moving the dogs into a big truck. The men all got into the truck and they sped off like the wind.

The truck had a fake sticker on it. It said BODE'S REMOVALS.

No one realised that BODE'S REMOVALS sticker was a fake. No one realised that BODE'S REMOVALS was not a real company. No one realised the truck had no numberplate. More important, the truck driver didn't know how to drive the truck.

The BODE'S REMOVALS truck drove past the police when Sammi and Jodie walked out. They recognised Mr Bode driving the truck.

"He... He... HIM! I think... THAT GUY! I KNOW HIM!!" Jodie yelled in utter amazement.

"Yes! Quick! Tell the police!" Sammi screeched. But Jodie was back inside the station before Sammi even finished her sentence. Jodie told the police about the BODE'S REMOVALS and what they thought it was.

"Thought?" The officer said.

Jodie sighed. "Look, please, if you just go after them and see," she pleaded.

The officer shook his head. But then he agreed to go after the truck. He went off in a police car with the sergeant.

Sammi and Jodie tipped the coins out of their pockets. They had $18.60. That was probably just enough money to get them to the airport. Sammi used the phone and called a taxi.

The trip to the airport cost $10.50. They had $8.10 left

The men had anaesthetised the dogs so they looked like teddies. The police were waiting at the check-in for the man.

When Mr Bode got to the check-in the police officer asked, "Can I please see your driver's licence, Sir?"

"Hmm..." Mr Bode thought about it. "Yes, officer." He pulled out his wallet which contained a fake licence.

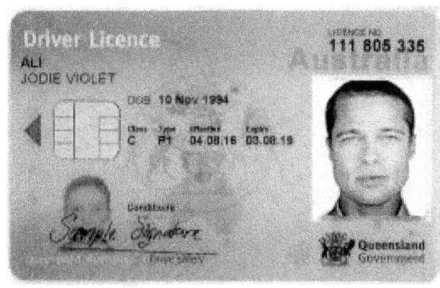

The office of frowned and studied the card. He shook his head and said, "No... no. Please can you and your friends bring your crates and come to the police car?" A few other police cars arrived and took the criminals away to prison!

Sammi and Jodie got a ride to their houses in the police car. They each got $150.

Jodie bought a teeny tiny Golden Labrador. She named it Waffle. Waffle had a fluoro pink collar. Sammi and Jodie took Waffle for a walk every day in the dog park. Waffle loved the doggy pool. She was good and always did her doo-doo in the right place.

Sammi bought heaps of paints and decorations for her bedroom. Sammi and Jodie painted one wall aqua and the rest white. They put up Chinese lanterns and rainbow flags. In the end, Sammi's room looked so cool.

The girls often talked about their adventure. They always had to re-tell it to people at school and people they met.

One sunny day, (which was one month after the men went to prison) Sammi looked at the newspaper. It read:

C.Bode And Friends Escape!

Chris Bode and his friends (stealing and breeding dogs - then sold illegally) have broken out from prison on 4 November 2016. No one knows how or what time it was. Unfortunately, Mr Fraser the mayor will no longer be mayor after being questioned by the police and then confessing he was involved in this "dog business."

Sammi sighed and rang Jodie.

"Hi," Sammi said.

"Hi," Jodie replied.

"Did you see the newspaper?"

"Oh yes! I did! It's very bad, isn't it?"

"Well Jodie, are you ready for another adventure?"

"Yes I am!"

© Jodie Barber (Aged 12)